CREEP FACTOR

Thirteen Deeply Creepy Short Horror Stories

AMANDA LUZZADER AND CHADD VANZANTEN

DEDICATION

Amanda dedicates this book to Melissa, the Queen of Horror, who won't be disturbed in the least by any of these stories.

Chadd dedicates this book to the scariest thing that ever happened to him: his children.

CONTENTS

STAGE TWO
Chadd VanZanten

You go through three stages when you start a new job.

Stage One is when you're invisible. Nobody's sure if getting to know you will be worth the effort, and in my case they're probably right. I'm short, kind of pale, zits. That's the worst thing—almost twenty-five and I still get zits. Lots of them.

Also, I'm shy.

Worse than shy, if you ask my mom. I'm what she calls "backwards."

"He's okay," she used to say when I'd start crying for no good reason when other kids came over, "he's just backwards."

Stage Two is when you get noticed. Maybe you're doing a good job. Maybe you're really lazy but you're funny or good looking. In Stage Two, you get invited to the reindeer games, if you want to put it that way. You can ask what someone thought of a new movie and then you go to lunch together. You text them. They text you back. I've only been to Stage Two a few times because I'm not good looking or funny.

Also, I don't do a very good job.

My dad used to say, "Son, you've got a problem with your eyesight: you can't picture yourself working too hard."

It's not my fault I get stuck in Stage One a lot. Not all my fault, I should say. The stage system was designed to keep people like me in Stage One. At other jobs I've actually been demoted from Stage Two back into Stage One.

"He's just not ready," they tell each other. That's what I imagine. "He's just not Stage Two material."

It's okay. I usually quit when that happens.

Stage Three is the top. Stage Threes decide who's in what stage. Everyone's trying to impress them. They run the reindeer games. If a Stage Three invites you outside for a smoke, or sends you a friend request, that's it: you're promoted to Stage Two. I have never been to Stage Three, obviously.

Even back in high school when I was making lopsided snow cones at the Supah Snow, I somehow let a bunch of sixteen-year-old girls keep me in Stage One for a whole summer.

I'd been working in the programming division at Barr-Kane for about three months when I realized I had a big problem. Barr-Kane's a little code farm in the business park by the airport. The pay was okay, but after three months, I was still in Stage One. Way too long. And the longer you're in Stage One, the harder it is to get out. And you've got to get out. You can't just stay in Stage One forever. Trust me about that.

And it's not just about having friends to go to lunch with. It's nice to have friends, but I'm talking about actual mental survival. Imagine a job where no one says ten words to you all week. Imagine having no one to back you up if you get blamed for something you didn't do. That's Stage One. You can stay there for a couple weeks, or maybe a couple months, but if I didn't make it out soon, I was gonna have to quit, move back home.

There were at least a couple people in my department who could help me. First, there was Dimitri. He's a celebrity. Stage Three all the way. He started working at Barr-Kane only seven weeks before me, but he's just so good looking. Olive skin, curly black hair, and funny. He was always so funny. Dimitri had this cat named Devastator, and he always told stories about how the cat can fight off dogs and take a shit in the toilet. He didn't even teach it, either. The cat just watched him and figured it out, I guess. He's got video.

Dimitri was nice to everyone, even me. Smart, too. He once told me that if you eat 32 ounces of yogurt while you're drunk, it will sober you right up. Something about how the fat molecules absorb alcohol. It can't be fat-free yogurt, obviously. So, I went and got a tub of yogurt and a fifth of vodka and tried it. Didn't really work that good—threw up all over my couch. But I did feel better after that. That's the kind of guy he was.

I had seen Dimitri put people in Stage Two just by remembering their names or laughing at what they said. If Dimitri laughs at your joke, that's it: you're in Stage Two. The problem was that he always had a crowd of people around him, which made him hard to get close to.

The other person was Holly, the assistant operations manager. She was what my dad would describe as "AB." All Business. She was pretty, but she was in Stage Three because she worked hard and she was always fair. To Holly, it didn't matter if you had zits (which I have) or oily hair (which I also have), as long as you worked hard (which I could maybe fake) she would treat you fair.

I figured my best ticket to Stage Two was Dimitri, but it turns out that was going nowhere. So, I started working on Holly. She always ate lunch in the break room at one o'clock, so that's what I started doing. I don't think she noticed. I tried to camouflage myself by bringing really different things to eat every day. I figured if I brought Cup Noodles every time, she'd notice. Cup Noodles have a very distinct smell. It was all real complicated—I wanted her to notice me, but I didn't want her to notice-notice, so I'd bring leftovers one day, then I'd bring a Hot Pocket, then switch it up with some fast food, then back to Hot Pockets. Sometimes I'd sit far away, other times closer. I kept track of everything in an Excel spreadsheet so that I didn't inadvertently fall into any patterns.

Also, I tried bumping into Holly in the stockroom. If I

saw her go in there, I'd wait a few seconds and then go in and get a DVD or some paper clips. She may have gotten a little suspicious about that. It's a small room, and I caught her glaring at me a couple times.

Then again, I got so many DVDs she must've thought I was backing up the whole network 4 gigabytes at a time. My whole desk was just blank DVDs and paper clips.

One day I saw Holly go in the stockroom with a big stack of stuff to copy. That's where the copier is, in the stockroom. So, I waited a little while and followed her in, and when I got there the copier was beeping. It was perfect.

"Uh oh," I said. "Looks like a paper jam. You want me to fix that?"

She said, "Go right ahead."

Turns out it was an easy fix—the stupid collating unit. If you want to make double-sided copies on the stockroom copier, never use the collating unit or it'll jam. I'd only been there for three months and I knew that. And she could have fixed it. A monkey could—there's a little screen that shows animations of what to do, step-by-step. I figure she let me do it because I was there—you know, let the peon do it. I maybe saved her from getting a little toner on her clothes, but it was really just a minor favor, and she wouldn't promote me to Stage Three just for a dinky thing like that. So, I figured I'd try to just chat with her a little. Build a little goodwill. Maybe open a door later on. You never know.

But Holly kept her headphones in. Bad sign. She didn't take out even one headphone, and I figured if I talked too much, she might play that headphone trump card, which is when you point to your headphones and shake your head, which is the universal sign for, "I don't need to talk to you because you're a fat little loser and you're still in Stage One. Also, you have zits."

This has happened to me before. It's one of the most humiliating experiences I can think of, and my life is really just one humiliating thing after another, so it's not like I don't know about humiliation. I do.

4

Like that girl on the bus last winter—she was wearing a T-shirt with the name of a band I like, and without thinking I went over and said, "Stereolab. Right on." She pointed to her headphones and shook her head with a little sneer. I wanted to evaporate. I wanted to kill her on the spot. I got off the bus at the next stop and I didn't make it back to work and I got fired from that job. They didn't even take me aside and say, "Rick, listen, this isn't working out." The guy fired me right there in front of the receptionist and everyone else as I walked in the door the next morning.

But the thing that stuck with me, the thing I remember and think about, is that little sneer from the girl in the Stereolab T-shirt.

So, Holly kept her headphones in. She was bobbing her head and pretending to read the papers she was waiting to copy. The copier was fixed, but I was still pretending to work on it, fiddling with the little doors and watching Holly for an opening of some kind.

She looked up and said, "How's it coming?"

"Oh, it's just about there," I said. And that was my opening. Before she looked away I said, "What are you listening to?"

She furrowed her brow like she couldn't hear me. She was getting ready to make the little sneer, the little head shake. Shit, man, I just knew it. I considered aborting, but I was going to quit anyway if things didn't get better, so I said it again, louder.

"What are you listening to?"

She said she was listening to Yo La Tengo. I got up from the printer.

"Yo La Tengo?" I said. "No way. They're my third favorite band right now. They're playing at Spooky's in a couple weeks. Did you know that?"

Without realizing it I had walked right up to her, within one foot. I was practically talking down her throat, and she was not okay with it. Personal space—another thing I'm not good at. I ran back to the printer and closed it up.

"All fixed," I said.

Here's my big mistake—I figure if two people have the same taste in music, it's at least a basis for friendship. Turns out that's just not true. I never learn.

The girl in the Stereolab T-shirt had looked right through me, like I was transparent. I pointed to her T-shirt, trying to show we had a connection. I assumed by wearing the T-shirt she owed a fellow fan some minimal level of respect, but she only saw that I was pointing at her boobs. She rolled her eyes and moved as far away as possible. She got off the bus right away, at the next stop. I did, too, but she just walked away. I doubt she even saw me.

Holly at least thanked me, so I tried to salvage something while she made her copies.

"So, are you really into Yo La Tengo?" I asked.

She didn't look up, didn't say a word. It was like she was mentally willing the machine to go faster than sixty-four copies per minute.

"Because I have an extra ticket to the show." A lie.

"Really," she said. She didn't ask, "Really?" She just said the word, "really."

"Sure," I said. "If you want it, it's yours." Considering that I didn't even have a ticket, I should have maybe worked that a different way, but at that point I didn't care. "Sure, we could meet up at the show. Not like a date. Just an arrangement, you know, we could just meet and I'll give it to you."

"What was your name?" she asked.

"Rick."

"Rick, look, here's the 'arrangement.' I have a boyfriend and he really, really hates it when guys flirt with me at work. I've seen things get ugly. So."

Boyfriends. Girls always think boyfriends are part lover, part Secret Service agent, but boyfriends are usually ambivalent about beating people up. They're not attack dogs. Even the thick-necked, bouncer-type guys know about felony assault and civil litigation.

Husbands—they're dangerous. Brothers, too. Relatives

can actually, literally get away with murder when it has to do with crimes of passion involving men who try to harm a wife or sister.

But boyfriends? I have never had a problem with boyfriends.

I figured Holly was probably lying about having a boyfriend anyway, and later on I confirmed it. Turns out there was no mention of a boyfriend on her profile, no couple selfies on her phone. Boyfriend photos taped to the mirror on her dressing table? Nope. And no aftershave or extra toothbrush in her bathroom. I don't know who this supposedly jealous and protective boyfriend was, but as far as I could tell, Holly wasn't even on birth control.

Also, I was right about Dimitri. He got me out of Stage One. Finally. We got to talking about reggae one afternoon and I let him rip a couple of my really obscure CDs, old stuff you can't get online. When a Stage Three borrows shit from you, that's it: you're in Stage Two.

But Dimitri kind of disappointed me at Holly's funeral. Actually, I guess they called it a memorial—they never did find her. But when it was Dimitri's turn, he said, "Holly was always nice to everyone," which is what everyone says, but no one seems to care if it's true or not.

Holly wasn't always nice, and she sure as hell wasn't nice to everyone. Someone said the same thing about the girl in the Stereolab T-shirt at her memorial. Turns out her name was Whitney.

7

WHAT GOES UP
Amanda Luzzader

Hey, you know of any jobs? I gotta find me somethin'. I thought about working the line at Lipzer again, but it's too fast for me. At my age, I gotta take it slow.

Loved my last job, though. Grounds custodian at the Fun Factory. Best job I ever had. I can smell it now—popcorn, cotton candy, corn dogs, and a whiff of cigarette smoke. That's the perfume of fun, tell you what. And the sounds. Man, that place had its own soundtrack—bells and dings, crowd screamin', screechin' brakes—it all mixes together into one big song, and I got the whole thing memorized. You'd think it'd change from day to day, but it don't. I could tell ya exactly when the tracks from King's Tower was gonna clang or when Kenny at the ball toss was gonna yell, "Three tries a dolla'!"

Best part was them little kids. Smile or wave to them and they'd smile and wave right back. Not like their parents. I'm just landscape to them, see, like a tree or somethin'. But them kids, you give 'em somethin' small, like a balloon or somethin'—them kids get so excited.

Worst part of that job, though? Teenagers. They're the ones stickin' gum all over the place. Like I'd see one of 'em with a cheek full, chewing it like cud. I knew sooner or later I'd

9

be prying it offa the handlebar of the Sky Rail.

We'd get these pretty young things. You know the type—ponytails so high they bounce when they walk. They'd clear half an acre to avoid me. Get these disgusted looks on their faces, like I just stepped in shit. First time one of them looked at me like that, I swear I checked behind me. Thought they must've seen somethin' dead or somethin'. Didn't realize they was lookin' at me that way. But they was.

Anyways, the boys was the real punks. They'd sidle up to a trashcan, but 'stead of usin' it they'd just drop their trash on the ground while lookin' me right square in the eye.

I'd just smile. See, I made it into a game. How many different colors could I sweep up in one spot. Let 'em be punks; I didn't care.

One day, these two young fellas step off the Aztec Adventure, laughin' and bumpin' into each other like two drunk hyenas. 'Cept I know they ain't drunk; they're just mean. I kinda turn my back to them while I'm sweeping up. See, I don't want no trouble. But one of them calls to me. This kid's got these big zits all over his face. He was ugly on the inside and the outside.

He yells to me, "Hey. Hey, retard!"

I don't turn around. Just keep on sweepin'—see, I don't want no trouble.

But next thing I know, one of them's thrown his soda cup at me. Hits me upside the head. Drips down my neck, all over my shirt.

"You missed one," says Ugly, and the two of them are really grabbing at each other, laughin' so hard they can barely breathe; faces turnin' all red.

I gripped my broom so tight, lucky it didn't snap in half.

Anyways, I bend over to pick up the cup. With these old knees, it ain't that easy getting' up and down. But I don't see when one of them sneaks up behind me. While I'm bent down, he takes his foot and shoves me over.

Skinned up my nose and chin. Maybe that don't sound so bad, but it was bleedin' pretty good and at my age I don't bounce back so fast no more. Three years on the job, and I'd never had so much as a paper cut 'til then. Ole Ugly and his pal are howlin', and I've never been so mad in my entire life.

But what can you do, you know? Can't do nothin'. Not a damn thing.

So, they finally head off, but I can't drop it this time. Really burnin' me up. I start emptying trashcans, but I'm jerking those bags around and smashing the garbage down; thinking the whole time what I'd like to do to them two little assholes. And the heat's just comin' off me like a bad sunburn.

Then, all a sudden, there's this horrible screech. And I knew right away something was wrong. 'Cause of the soundtrack, you know? Like there's feedback on the recording. So, I look over, and we've got this giant roller coaster. They call it The Almighty. Third tallest loop in the nation. And them cars have stopped right at the very top, people all upside down there with their hair hanging. And I seen them two punks in the very front seats. Recognized 'em' cause they had these colorful shirts, see, but I swear I can almost see ole Ugly's zits from where I'm standing.

So, I'm just watching them stuck there and suddenly, I can't hear the soundtrack no more. All I hear is my own heartbeat. It's beating faster and louder. Faster and louder. And all that anger inside me, it becomes this physical thing. Like I could take it outta me and hold it. Or I could send it off somewhere. Somewhere else, somewhere far away.

And I'm thinking about this, this anger and where it could go, and then I hear a "click," clear as day. It's a "click," like a seat belt coming undone. And I look up at The Almighty, and their restraints have failed. Not all the cars, mind you, just them two nasty little boys.

And they tumble on out.

What a strange sensation that musta been for 'em. They tumble up outta their seats towards the ground below. Upside down but flyin' up to the concrete sky.

So they tumble out but somehow they grab onta something and they're hanging on for dear life. Big Ugly is hanging onta the seat or the car somehow, and his little buddy is hanging onta Ugly.

People start runnin' around and screamin'. I'm just calm, lookin' at them boys looking like that they's monkeys in that barrel 'o monkeys game. Finally, the little one drops. He was hanging onta Ugly, but he drops. Wouldn't be surprised if ole Ugly shucked him off and let him drop. Ugly's up there all alone now, and he's grabbin' and pullin' and for second there I think he's gonna get holda something and climb back up to safety.

But he don't.

Makes this sound when he hits, kinda quiet, but I could hear it. Anyways, you don't have to see to know how it all ended.

That's when I knew why them girls was always so 'fraid of me. See? Cuz, I don't know how I did it. But I did, you know? Don't know how, but I did. So, I had to quit. Just couldn't risk nobody else gettin' hurt. Too many teenage jerks at these amusement parks these days.

Anyways, you hear of any job openings, could you let me know? Maybe somethin' with little kids. I really like little kids.

CHIEFTAIN
Chadd VanZanten

Dogs do the craziest things. They sniff each other's butts, lick their genitals. They hump your leg—they'll hump a couch cushion. They're the craziest animals ever. Except monkeys, maybe, drinking their own pee and playing with themselves at the zoo. But dogs are right up there, crazy-wise.

They bark and bark and bark, which is not crazy by itself—it's how they communicate—but they'll bark for hours and hours. The Rottweiler that lived at the green house up the street barked all night long. Ten, twelve hours. What was he trying to accomplish? They kept him on a chain, inside a fenced yard. Maybe that had something to do with it. Still, after the first couple hours, you'd think he'd give up. He never did. This was an animal with the ability to lick his own testicles, but he chose to bark for ten hours in a row. Tell me that's not crazy.

A few years ago, I was in the garage with my dad when our dog wandered in. His name was Topper. Irish setter. He was pretty old at the time but still very enthusiastic about the testicle-licking thing, so he came in and sat there licking himself. I mean he went at it for five or ten minutes. My dad was in the middle of something—letting some lacquer dry or something. So we just sat there as Topper licked himself.

Finally, I looked at my dad. He looked at me and shrugged.

"He's getting old. There's less and less for him to do around here."

So then Topper spotted some used-up sandpaper by the workbench and started chewing on it.

I looked at my dad again.

He looked at Topper and said, "All dogs love sandpaper. Nobody knows why."

Can anybody really understand dogs for sure? Or any animal? A dog will eat its own vomit—can't be a good reason for that. And they're fixated on excrement. They eat it, roll in it, search it out wherever they go.

Me and my girlfriend Brenda used to take Topper to the dog park. We'd sit watching the other dogs, and every single one would either be making shit, eating shit, or smelling each other's asses. Barking and sniffing each other's asses. And if they like what they smell, they'll give a little lick—just a tender little lick on the anus. Is that a compliment?

Of course, I can't actually watch any other dogs anymore. You need eyes for watching things. Nowadays, I just listen. I take my dog Bowser. He's a black lab. People call him a "seeing-eye dog," but the proper term is "guide dog."

Brenda left me not long after the attack. She said, "I can't stand to see you this way," and then I guess she realized how that came out, and she went sprinting out of the hospital and that was pretty much the last time I spoke with her.

So, my little sister Lucy comes along now, so we can let Bowser out of his harness to run around.

Bowser's a working dog. I'm not supposed to let people pet him or socialize with him. And it's not because he'll bite or bark, it's because he's on duty, and he's not supposed to play on the job. It'll mess up his focus, his training. But he won't bite. He rarely even barks or growls. He's very steady, very well trained.

But that's one thing dogs do that's not crazy at all—they

growl. There's only one reason dogs growl: to put fear into another creature. They have that ability. They can create fear. They can create that black fog of midnight inside your brain. At any time of the day.

They're predators, or they were way back in olden times. Wolves, basically. All the dogs we have today are descended from wolves. The big ones the small ones. Chihuahuas, wiener dogs—all of them come from wolves, and wolves are wild. They growl for a real reason. Like when two wolves want the same piece of moose leg, they growl to scare each other away. Whichever one growls loudest or best wins, I guess.

When wolves chase prey, they growl to make the prey afraid, so that black fog will take over and they'll make a mistake. That's the key—the prey makes a mistake.

A few years ago, I read about a lady who got killed by some kind of pit-bull and I thought, "Come on, lady. It's a dog. Stand up for yourself. Fight it off. Sure, it can bite you, but it can't kick or throw a punch or use strategy. Even big dogs only weigh a hundred pounds or so. It's not a grizzly bear—just fight the thing off."

But it's really not that easy. Not in the dark, when you're not expecting it.

Like when it's midnight. You're walking home from your girlfriend's house. Got your hands in your pockets because it's a little chilly out. You're coming to the green house up the street and you think, "I wonder why that stupid dog isn't barking its stupid head off tonight?"

The owners shout his name all the time—it's Sergeant or Caesar or something like that, but you're thinking about your girlfriend and how her lotion rubbed off on your sweater and it smells good, but you had a fight with her. She's upset because her aunt had to have a radical mastectomy.

She says, "And my Uncle Phil is leaving her. Can you believe that?"

Guys, if your girlfriend asks you something like that, do not shrug. Whatever you do or say, do not shrug. Because she'll say, "What does that mean? That shrug. You're okay if a guy leaves his wife just because she had to have her boobs cut off?"

"No," you say. "I didn't mean anything. I just shrugged."

And she'll say, "I know what you did. So what if my boobs got cut off. Would you leave me?"

And then you say, "Brenda. Babe, quit. I'm not saying I'd leave you. I'm saying boobs are important."

Her mouth literally falls open.

"Not to me," you say. "But, Uncle Phil, obviously."

And that's why it's midnight and you're walking home with your hands in your pockets, and that's why the smell of your girlfriend's lotion is going to be on your sweater a lot longer than she's going to be your girlfriend.

Because when you pass by the green house you think, "Why isn't that dog barking its stupid head off, and why is the gate on that fence open?"

That's when you hear the jingling. Just a little jingle. From the ID tags on the dog's collar. You've heard it before, and in a way it's kind of pretty, but you've always heard it coming from inside of the fence. Never this close, never this clearly, never from behind you.

So you turn around and see the dog. Just a blur, really, because it's dark and you're still kinda thinking about Brenda. But the collar is jingling and the dog is blurring and now words pop into your mind, words you don't think about very often.

Words like "fang" and "artery."

Then the dog growls. It's a heavy sound, an impressive sound. It's way better than any sound effect in any movie. You think, "That growl is for me. He wants me to make a mistake."

It works. You somehow get your hands free of your pockets and your arms fly up to protect yourself, but what are you doing to do? He's a hundred and ten pounds and he's already in the air. Before you know it you're on your back and your head goes crack on the pavement and your vision goes white and the dog gets in real close.

Then you remember—Chieftain. The dog's name is

Chieftain. You think, this is somebody's pet, somebody's pal. You've heard the lady who lives in the green house ask this dog, "Who's a good boy?"

You try to fend him off but Chieftain is quick, and his big hot head plunges between your hands. His mouth opens. He's going right for your face, right for your eyes.

That's when you think, this dog isn't crazy. He knows exactly what he's doing.

POWER COUPLE
Amanda Luzzader

I've had other girls, sure. I've had girlfriends and crushes and flings. I had a torrid love affair once. I've had friends with benefits, and one time I even had an enemy with benefits. I've had some of the most excellent girlfriends a guy like me could ask for.

But none of them were like Julia.

None of them were even close. Julia was on a whole other scale. Just thinking about her made my heart want to explode, and it affected other parts of my body, too. So it's hard to say what I liked so much about her. Hard to say what it was I couldn't do without.

Which I guess is why I knew I had to end it. I had to break up with her.

Julia was beautiful. Sure she was. Best looking girl I ever went out with—by far. Long, silvery, blond hair, delicate features, and almond-shaped eyes that I thought at first were gray but she told me were hazel. I'd never gone out with someone with hazel eyes. They had a way of piercing you, hypnotizing you. And with the combination of the eyes and Julia's high cheekbones, the description that always came to my mind was "barbarian princess." She had that kind of wild, barbarian look to her, only more fine, more delicate.

Oh, and apparently she had eyebrows that other girls would die for. When I showed my sister Madeline a pic of Julia, she said, "Oh my god, this girl's got fierce brow game."

I agree with the fierce part. Making out with Julia was like making out with a small, savage creature. She didn't just kiss, she pushed into me, consumed me, wrapped around me like the ivy vines on the walls of the Student Center. She was strong. And tall.

Being with Julia was intoxicating, addictive. Like the smoothest liquor, the best drug. I didn't think I could ever get enough of her. And it's crazy how much and how often I thought of her—sometimes it was nonstop. Julia this. Julia that. It started as soon as I got up in the morning. I'd get up and think, "Which shirt will she like best? And which shoes?" I'd sit in my Origins of Man class and think, "What would Julia think of Professor Ashpodel? He's so uptight."

And the funny thing is, I felt like someone else when I was with her. She really did make me better. When I was by myself, no one noticed me or wanted to know anything about me. But when I was with Julia, we were like one of those power-couples. She made my stock go up. We were more than the sum of our totals.

I know I'm being all calm about this, but I was devastated that it couldn't last.

Kelton told me, "You need to make your move, bro." Kelton's my best friend. He said: "She's hot, she's smart, she's seriously and completely out of your league, and she's into you. You never stop talking about her, so make your move. Marry her. Move in with her. Whatever, bro. Figure out your move and play it."

I should mention that Julia had a dark side. For some reason she reminded me of a rainy day, or a day when it seems like it should be raining but it isn't. And I loved that about her, too.

Madeline once told me, "I actually find her a little intimidating."

"Really?" I said. "Julia intimidates you?"

"No, I guess maybe intimidating isn't the right word," she said. "Imposing?"

"I can see that," I said, though I thought the word "bewitching" might be better.

But that's not why I had to break up with her. It had been a mistake to let things go so far with Julia. To let things progress that way. That's the thing. I knew I was falling for her. Sure I did. God knows why she fell for me, but I knew that was happening, too. I should have put a stop to it earlier, like with the others. Wendy, for instance, was so good to me, would do anything for me, but as soon as I realized she wanted to make things permanent, that was my signal. I put an end to it. Carla was stunning, especially when she wore an up-do and showed cleavage, but I ended that right after the third date. Brit made me laugh every time we talked. She was so smart, so funny—I dumped her. And all the others—Brooklyn, Katheryn, Kaci, Katy, Sammy, Sariah, Mariah, Marianne, Joanne, Jaqueline. I broke it off whether I wanted to or not.

I couldn't make exceptions. Julia was the best I'd ever had, but there could be no exceptions. I looked at my calendar. First Monday in June. I'd end it before that.

I told Kelton. I told Madeline.

"Well," sighed Madeline. "It's your life. Ruin it however you want to ruin it."

"Your brain is messed up, bro," said Kelton. "What, do think she's too good for you?"

They were both kind of right. Sure they were. Madeline thought I'd ruin my life if I let Julia go. What she doesn't understand is that my life is already so complicated, you could say it's ruined already.

Look, I know that I'm only a five or five-and-a-half on the boyfriend scale. On a good day, when my hair looks good and I'm wearing a favorite shirt, you might catch me thinking of myself as a six, but that's where I top out. And I realize looks aren't everything—but I also have no money. I deliver pizza and I'm a history major with student loans. I don't know how it happened, but I don't see myself on the super fast track to fabulous wealth.

And all the other things that might compensate for my lack of looks and money? Yeah, I don't have those, either. Natural leader? Nah. Hopeless romantic? Please. Snappy dresser? Take another look. Sensitive? Ambitious? Deeply empathic? Artistic? Rich inner life? None of the above.

I can't even cook.

I'm not saying Kelton is exactly right, either—that Julia's too good for me. I think every person should have a say in who is too good for who, and Julia would never say that she's too good for me. In fact, she said the opposite on a regular basis.

"I'm so lucky I found you," she once said to me. I am not making this up.

But there are things Julia doesn't know about me, big, important, complicated things, things I just cannot tell her, and that makes it unfair. You have to know everything about a person before you can make an informed decision about whether you're too good for that person.

See, I've got a dark side, too. I don't mean I brood and smolder like Julia. I've actually done things. I've got priors. And I'd be crushed if Julia ever found out. So, it's not exactly that Julia's too good for me, it's that she doesn't realize that she deserves someone better. But I do. Sure I do. She deserves better. And yeah, maybe I top out at six-and-a-half or seven on the boyfriend scale, and yeah, maybe that's only because I'm decent in bed, but I've got a heart, and I'm at least a half-decent human being, and so I'm making the call on Julia's behalf.

Kelton: "You're an idiot, bro. You're an idiot. You're an idiot. You're an idiot"

Madeline: "You need to think about this. For a long time. Like a really long time."

They don't understand. They don't understand me because they don't really know me, either. Of course they don't. Not completely. Because if they did, they would understand, and I'd like that, but I'd hate it, too. Because they'd want nothing to do with me, either, just like Julia if she knew. How terrible would that be—my sister and best friend and my girlfriend? No. It's got to stop. I marked it down. It was on the calendar. First Monday in June.

But there was a problem. We had a date, me and Julia. I'm usually so good with keeping track because this girl Kerry I dated for a while showed me how to use Google Calendar. At first I thought it was stupid, but after I broke up with her I started looking into it more closely and I honestly don't know how I survived without an online calendar. I mean this in a very literal sense. A guy like me really plans everything on a monthly basis, right down to the hour. It was a perfect fit.

So, I have no idea how this happened, but I forgot to put down that I was going to the goddam Parade of Homes with Julia on—you guessed it—the first Sunday in June.

You may not know what the Parade of Homes is. It's not an actual parade. There are no floats or anything. It's just this home decor thing where people buy tickets to go to the ritzy part of town and walk through all the rich people's McMansions. I know, I know, it's messed up—all the broke-ass people pay the people who already have plenty of money to go and look in their houses.

But I never miss it. I go every year.

I don't care about floor runners or staircase finials or intelligent shower heads. I hear people say "pergola" a lot when I go. I don't know what that is.

I have my own reasons for going to "The Parade," thank you very much. Let's just say I'm a big fan of home security systems and I like to check the latest technology in broad daylight, especially in that particular neighborhood. Here's the problem: a white, male, impoverished history major who ranks (at the very maximum) seven or eight on the boyfriend scale has a way of seeming, I dunno—odd? out of place?—when attending The Parade unaccompanied.

That's why I always need a date. And I had one for this year. I just forgot to put it down in my Google Calendar.

"You really want to go?" I asked Julia.

"Omigod, yes," she said. "I've been looking forward to it since April."

This was terrible. I needed to be done with Julia before that Monday. Not just for my sake—for her's, too. Ideally, it'd be several days before, and even better would be a week before. But breaking up one day beforehand could present certain complications—again, for Julia and me both. I had no interest in ruining my own enjoyment of The Parade—I planned on many happy returns, and breaking up with Julia was gonna be the worst break-up ever. I didn't want the two associated.

But what could I do?

I picked up Julia at 10 a.m. sharp. I didn't want to be late. There were so many promising homes this year and I wanted to see them all, but I was also filled with a sense of dread. Walking around The Parade with my very-soon-to-be-best-ex-girlfriend-ever gave me a deeply conflicted feeling, and Julia could tell.

"Derek, what's the matter with you today?" she said. "Did I do something to upset you? It seems like something's wrong."

"No, babe," I told her. "Everything's okay. Whoa, look at these motion sensors. The emitters are so tiny, but they cover the entire yard. SafeT4U has really upped their game."

All the homes had incredible new systems that year. It was the year Maximum Klaxon launched the Earsplitter900. KeepEmOut Inc had a new high-rez doorbell cam. And Happy-Taze was showing the latest in wall-mounted household tazing devices.

But I couldn't hide from Julia.

"Why don't you just call me later, okay?" she said. "Something's obviously wrong, but since you won't tell me, I'm gonna go."

I pulled her into a brand new panic room. It was gorgeous—tasteful paneling, a 52-inch Sony. And it had that "new panic room smell."

But I told her: "You're right, babe. I'm sorry. I should just be straight with you. This isn't working out."

"What?" Her face went pale. "Derek, what is it? What did I do? What happened?

I tried to tell her that it wasn't her, it was me—and I really meant it. It was me, obviously. I couldn't be with someone. Every 29-and-a-half days I could barely be with myself. I wasn't happy about it. I wanted to be with Julia. I wanted to be normal.

But that wasn't how it was.

"Derek, you're making a mistake," she said. "We belong together. I know it. I know you. And I love you."

That really hurt. I'd said the words I was about to say to Julia a gajillion times to other girls. Sure I had. But that doesn't mean it ever got easier, and with Julia it was the worst ever.

"Jules," I said, clearing my throat and taking a deep breath, "listen to me. I don't want to be with you. I don't want to see you again, ever. I don't want to talk to you or text you or even e-mail." People never e-mail anymore, I know, but you'd be surprised what a girl who's had her heart broken by a guy who is at best an eight-and-a-half will do to un-break it.

Julia stared at me, the fierceness of her hazel eyes softened by her sadness. Thick, gooey tears quivered in her eyes and rolled down her face. And she ran away. My barbarian princess was gone.

I didn't finish The Parade. My heart wasn't in it anymore, and there wasn't a lot of time, anyway. So, I went to the Safeway, bought 40 pounds of beef, went to my apartment, and took off all my clothes.

As the sun went down and the sky in the east began to glow with the silvery light of the moon rise, I thought about Julia. Some of my other breakups had been difficult to get past, difficult to forget. I'd say that Julia would be the hardest to forget, but that'd be wrong.

I'd never forget Julia. Of course I wouldn't.

Then there was a knock at the door. It was a soft knock at first. This had happened to me before. I'd always arranged my schedule so that, aside from the occasional stray Mormons, I'd never be visited at this time of the lunar cycle. The few random people who'd blundered into knocking on my door at this pivotal moment would either end up as a meal, or they go away after a few minutes. But I knew this was no random person.

The knock got louder, and then I heard her voice.

"Derek? Open up. I know you're there."

You see what I mean now. Girls will do nutty things after a breakup. That's why the date was so dicey. That's why I needed to end it before. Breakups sometimes have a transitional zone, where you're neither together nor broken up. Anything could happen.

But I couldn't see her. Not now, and not anytime within the next twenty-four hours. I waited.

"Derek, I can hear you."

Bullshit. I was on the couch twelve feet from the door, sitting utterly still, and barely breathing. She'd have a better chance hearing a mouse crawling along the baseboard in the next room.

"Derek, I know you're there, and if you don't open this door, I'll do something crazy. I'll call the cops or your sister. Or I'll break down this goddam door. I can do it."

Psh. Break down a solid-core red-oak laminate security door with a Klapco D-29 deadbolt? Not likely. But she might call Madeline. That could get awkward in a hurry. I glanced out the window. I had maybe thirty minutes. Definitely no more than that, and very likely less—the change wasn't exactly something you could set a watch by.

I fastened the door-restricting chain and opened the door as much as it could go—only about an inch. Then I peered through the space. Julia had been crying—I could tell that from her voice, but now I could see her eyes were reddened and her face was blotchy.

"You're a liar, Derek," she said, a little sob catching in her voice. "You want to be with me and you know it."

"You need to leave, Julia," I said, my voice breaking. "We're through. For good. I'm closing this door and you're gonna go home." My skin was getting warm and itchy. My teeth and gums ached. I didn't have time for this.

"No," said Julia, her voice suddenly low and imposing. "You're going to let me in."

I almost did, too. I almost unlatched the chain and opened the door to let her in. Her voice had changed. And then I looked at her eyes, and they were changed as well. Her face wasn't blotchy from crying—she was transforming.

I fumbled with the door chain, but my fingers were thickening, growing gnarled and hairy. By the time I got it unlatched and swung the door open, half of Julia's clothing lay in tatters on the entryway of my apartment. In another moment or two, we stood before each other, two animals, two Children of the Night.

With her sleek coat, brilliant flashing fangs, and exquisite tail, she was even more beautiful now than I'd ever seen her. I guess you could say we got back together that night.

I don't know how many girlfriends I'd had. A couple dozen, I guess. Playing the odds that way, this was bound to happen—sooner or later I was sure to find someone to really love, someone I could be myself with. I'd never thought about it, had never watched for it, but I knew I'd never need to find a date for The Parade ever again.

We stood there in the middle of my apartment for a moment, circling one another. And then, as if there'd been some signal only we could hear, we embraced in a fearsome animalistic embrace that would have torn any mortal girl or guy to pieces. We sank to the floor, sank into one another, and were consumed with the wildest of beastly passion deep into the midnight as the moon beamed in through the windows.

Hours later, as we lay entwined on the floor, I saw the hunger in Julia's eyes. I was starving, myself. I'd never waited so long to feed. I'd decided to stay in my apartment that night and try to be content with the raw grocery store beef I'd stacked neatly on my kitchen table. Julia briefly regarded it with obvious distaste, and then she looked back at me.

Her hazel eyes said, "Let's run together into the night, and we'll feed."

And so we did.

LAURA LEE HARTFORD
Chadd VanZanten

Russell walks along the beach in the place where he once lived, not too far from where he grew up. A lot has changed since he moved away. The roads are wider and the cars go faster, but the beach is still mostly the same. When he squints his eyes, he sees the town as it once was, and this makes him feel happy. And sad, too.

He comes to the sprawling pier. The sun shines bright on the planks of the docks and boardwalks, and waves smash into the pilings. People stroll among the shops and chowder houses.

Two ladies sit together on a bench. As Russell passes by, he recognizes one of them. The realization is so poignant, it's almost like a voice in his head says, "Russell, wait. That's Laura Lee Hartford."

Russell slows down and glances back, but he can't be sure of anything, so he keeps walking. He doesn't want to embarrass himself, so he walks all the way to the end of the pier and looks at the sea awhile. Gulls and seabirds are hovering and diving over the shrinking tide. Russell watches them, but he can almost feel her presence behind him. Laura Lee Hartford. He turns around and leans against the rail with his back to the water. She's still there, laughing and talking.

After a few moments more, Russell walks back in the direction of the two ladies. Not in the direction of Laura Lee Hartford—in the direction of the two ladies. Because it can't be her. Here, just sitting by the sea after all these years on the day he has returned to town? He walks in her direction, but slowly. He wants to know if it's her but he doesn't want to know that it's not her. He wants the realization to dawn slowly. He walks by the bench.

It's her. It's Laura Lee Hartford.

I can't believe this, thinks Russell. He turns and pauses by an iron lamp post, crouches to tie his shoe, and takes a longer look.

Laura Lee Hartford! He stands and chuckles to himself. Oh, if you only knew how low you brought me, he thinks.

But she doesn't know. Russell never talked to her after she moved out all those years ago, never told her how he dropped out of college and then just drifted for a long time.

Laura Lee stands and gives her friend a goodbye hug, then she gathers her glossy paper shopping bags and walks away alone. As Russell watches her, memories flash by like billboards seen from a speeding car. He remembers miniature golf with her. Long walks along the estuary. Bird watching.

She's not the twenty-year-old girl Russell fell in love with. She has a bit of grey hair and a few wrinkles, though of course Russell would never think of mentioning anything like that.

That was my main problem, he thinks. Too polite, too timid. I didn't let her know how I really felt. Didn't want to be presumptuous.

"Russell, say something to her." Again, the impression is so strong it's almost like an actual voice.

I'm too embarrassed, he thinks, shocked to discover how much he still hurts, how strong his feelings have remained.

Russell says nothing, but he follows Laura Lee at a distance along the pier, shadows her right into a small candy shop. That's right, Russell recalls, Laura Lee loves her candy. He thinks back to the night of the sweetheart's ball and heart-shaped box of chocolates he gave her. It was just grocery store candy. Nothing special. But it made her smile. She kissed him. Then they went to a dance, and afterwards, when they made love, her mouth tasted like cordial cherries.

In the candy shop, an old man makes cotton candy. His eyes are frosted with cataracts. He makes the cotton candy mostly by touch, but each plume is perfect. The blind candy man is a local novelty, and tourists crowd into the store. Russell scoots right next to the woman he knew, the woman he loved. He stands just a little behind her, close enough to catch the scent of her hair. She smells much like he'd remembered.

Laura Lee buys a cotton candy. While the old man makes change for her, she pulls off a tuft and places it in her mouth. Before her lips close, Russell sees the cotton candy begin to melt on her tongue.

Ashamed to have noticed her grey hair, Russell wonders which of his imperfections Laura Lee would notice first. He hasn't aged anywhere nearly as well as she has. His hair is almost gone now, and all around his eyes there are wrinkles and droopy skin.

Russell watches her leave with her cotton candy and shiny shopping sacks. He watches her turn and continue down the boardwalk, but this time he can't bring himself to follow her.

"Cotton candy or something else?" asks the old man.

Russell blinks. The old man holds a fresh paper stick, ready to twirl it through machine's windy chamber.

"No," says Russell. "I have diabetes."

"Ah. Just lookin', huh?"

"Well, no," stammers Russell. "It's just—this is dumb. There was a girl here, a woman. The one who was just here, just walked out. I used to know her. I was going to say hello, but it's been so long."

"How long?" asks the old man, grinning blindly.

The man in line behind Russell clears his throat testily.

"Oh, golly," laughs Russell, "twenty-five years? Going on thirty, I guess. We went to college here. That's where we met."

"But you got one look at her after all that time and

flipped out and couldn't talk to her. That it?"

"Yeah," says Russell. "I guess that really is it. But it's a small town—I'm sure I'll see her again."

"Know what I think? I think if you're not gonna buy some cotton candy off me, you oughta go talk to her."

Russell laughs again. "I guess I ought to. Sorry. Thanks. I'll be back. She loves candy."

He hustles out of the store and spots Laura Lee near the place where the pier meets the street. There's a parking lot there. She must be heading to her car. Russell breaks into a trot.

"Laura Lee," he cries, running faster. "Laura Lee, wait up."

When he catches up to her, she turns around and looks a little startled.

"Laura Lee," he pants. "It's me, Russ. Sorry, didn't mean to scare you, but I saw you back there on the boardwalk and I just got in town and I—I just wanted to say hi. How have you been?"

She answers with a smile. Her eyes crinkle in a familiar, friendly way, and her teeth are straight and white. Russell's heart breaks all over again, but it doesn't hurt. This time it almost feels good. This time it feels right.

"I'm sorry," she says. "You've got the wrong person. Did you run all the way down the pier?"

"No, Laura Lee, it's me, Russell. Russell Banks, from school. We had an apartment just right over here."

"No," she says, shaking her head, "that's not my name."

He moves closer. The shopping bags crackle as she backs away.

"Please," she says, "you've got the wrong person."

She hurries into the parking lot, clawing at her purse for her car keys. Russell follows, not knowing quite what to say. He grabs her arm but she shouts and jerks away from him and dives into her car. She dials a phone as she speeds away, and Russell is alone.

"Russell, that was her," says the voice. "You know it

was."

"I know. I know. But why then?" pleads Russell. "Why would she act that way?"

"Because she doesn't know how hard you took it. She must have heard from your friends or your sister."

"But I never blamed her," says Russell. "She doesn't have to pretend she doesn't know me. To run away."

"Russell. She's the reason you came back. It's time for you to admit that. You dropped everything and came all the way here to find her and somehow you did. You can't just let her go."

"Yeah," he breathes. "I guess you're right."

Russell goes back to the pier, finds a shopkeeper who'll let him use a phone book, and flips through it until he finds her address. He goes to her house, a tall split-level in the coastal hills overlooking the sea. At the front door, he breathes deeply, straightens his shirt collar, and knocks.

A man answers.

Russell was half expecting this, and he was ready for it. He thinks, "It has been a long time, after all, but it still hurts." The man is tall and seems friendly. So, thinks Russell, she settled down. A newspaper dangles from the man's fingertips. In a voice as steady as he can manage, Russell tells the man he would like to speak with Laura Lee.

"Laura Lee," says the man slowly, a finger to his lips. "Well, there's no Laura Lee here." He smiles politely, adjusts his glasses. "You sure you have the right house number? The streets here are numbered a little crazy."

"I'm sure," says Russell, a strained smile on his lips. "I grew up over in Stafford. I know the area well. Tell her I'm sorry about earlier. Tell her I just want to talk for a minute. It wouldn't have to be alone or anything. You could stay with us. I'm an old friend."

Then Russell sees Laura Lee coming down the stairs to the landing. She has light-colored, flannel pajamas on. Bare feet. She tries to peer over the man's shoulder, but he blocks the opening with his body.

"If that's the pesticide guy," she says, "I've got a check for him."

The man turns to whisper to her, keeping himself between her and Russell. The man hands her his newspaper, then steps onto the porch and swings the door shut behind him.

"What's going on?" Russell asks.

The man puts his hand on Russell's shoulder and tries to lead him to the sidewalk.

"Anyway," he says, "it seems like you really do have the wrong address, so--"

Russell shoves him away, shoves him so hard his glasses fall off into the grass. He retreats from Russell with one finger held up to warn him back, but Russell advances. The man gets inside his house and somehow manages to keep Russell out.

There is shouting, broken glass. Porch lights wink on and neighbors appear. The police arrive. They handcuff Russell, drive him to a station, sit him at a table in a little room. They leave him there for an hour. Then, outside in the hallway, a police officer and a detective approach the door and stop there.

"Apparently," says the officer, "he roughed up a tourist at the pier earlier today. We sent a unit but they couldn't find him. Two hours later he's hassling some guy and his wife up in the neighborhoods. That's where they grabbed him. Simple battery on both. Busted a window at the house. No permanent address in twenty-some years. Warrants and paroles in other states. I printed you a copy. Victims' statements are in there, too."

The detective leafs through a manila folder. "Thanks, Stu," she says, peering through the small window of Russell's holding cell. "'Preciate it. How's he doing right now? Do you know?"

"Pretty quiet," says the officer. "He seems kinda spaced out. He won't give you any trouble, I don't think. He's cuffed. I'm heading home, but you can call my cell phone if you have any questions."

"I'll get him booked."

The detective comes into the room carrying the file folder. She straightens her jacket, sits at the desk. Russell stares at his hands and the nickel-plated handcuffs. She opens the file.

"Hello—Russell," she says. "Sorry to keep you waiting so long. Looks like you've had a busy day. How you holding up?"

"Russell, it's her. It's Laura Lee Hartford."

Russell looks up, squints his eyes.

She smiles.

She's not the twenty-year-old Russell fell in love with, but her eyes crinkle in that familiar, friendly way, and her teeth are straight and white. Russell's heart breaks again, but it doesn't hurt. This time it almost feels good. This time it feels right

LARRY IS A LUMP
Amanda Luzzader

Steph bolted upright. Her pillow fell off the bed. She clutched the neck of her nightgown.

"Larry," she whispered, eyes wide, straining to see in the darkness. She shook his shoulder. "Larry!"

"Jeeze," murmured Larry.

"Larry," she hissed. "Wake up, dammit!"

"I'm awake," said Larry, a testy edge in his voice. He propped himself up on an elbow. "Whaddya want?"

"I heard something."

Larry sighed.

"A noise. I think someone's in the house."

They held still.

"What kinda noise?" Larry finally asked.

"I don't know. It woke me up." Steph's shoulders tightened and she leaned closer to Larry. "Go check it out."

Larry put his head back on the pillow. "Probably a dream."

"No, listen. It woke me up." Even with her night eyes, Steph couldn't see much. She stared at a dark shadow against the wall.

"I'm tired," Larry groaned. "You sure it wasn't the cat?"

"The cat?"

"Yeah," he said. "We own a cat. He plays all night."

Steph licked her dry lips. "No. I let him out."

"I don't think so," Larry said.

"This wasn't a cat sound. It was the sound of someone moving around. A squeak, maybe. Like the floor squeaking."

"Calm down," he muttered. "Just take a breath and go back to sleep.

Steph retrieved her pillow then wrapped her arms around herself, elbows close to her sides. She felt her heartbeat in her ears and at the back of her throat.

"Larry, can you just check? Just to put my mind at east?"

"I don't think so. It'll just encourage you. It was the cat. Go to sleep."

She sat there, body tense. Larry rolled over and lay there like a lump.

Was that a noise? Was it the sound of a cat on a hardwood floor? Or was it the soft hiss of fabric as someone moved in the darkness? Was there something there in the shadow? There in the black? Movement?

Larry's breathing eased into the soft sighs of sleep.

"Larry," said Steph, her voice high and tense. "I really think I let the cat out."

"Actually, you didn't," said a deep voice at the foot of the bed. "But don't worry, I did."

.

BIGGER
Chadd VanZanten

The film "Big" is not some kind of cinematic classic. Don't pretend like it is. It's got Tom Hanks in it and people like it, I know, but it's just a dinky little so-called comedy-adventure about a little boy who wishes he were big instead of short and scrawny. That's it. That's the whole thing.

It was directed by Penny Marshall, who was until 1988 best known for being one half of "Laverne and Shirley." I forget which half. Doesn't matter. What matters is this film really should have been bigger. Let me explain.

Oh: Spoiler Alert.

The film opens on the boy at a traveling carnival on Long Island, where he's in line to ride the Ferris wheel but discovers that he is too short to be permitted on the ride. A girl he likes is in line, too, and she sees him and laughs at him. He gets angry, runs away, and finds an antiquated arcade game containing a mechanized genie. The boy puts a coin in the machine and the automaton tells the boy to make a wish.

"I want to be big," he says.

In their minds, the viewers reply, "Yes. So do I." Maybe not taller, but just bigger and better than they are presently. And, obviously, that's why the movie works on any level at all--

we all want that. We all want to be bigger in some way.

Next morning the boy has the body of a 30-year-old man. Just like that. I have to admit that's kinda cool. But then it's a fairly predictable comedy of errors. Little boy in a big body, big world. He hides in Manhattan while his best friend searches for the genie arcade game so that the wish can be undone. Meantime, the boy tackles grown-up situations like dating a jaded New Yorker and dealing with a co-worker who's a dick, but when they find the genie arcade game, the man wishes himself back into to boy, who returns home to his devastated mother. Roll credits.

There are some tender moments in the film, such as when Tom Hanks touches his girlfriend's breast for the first time. The girlfriend is played by Elizabeth Perkins and she does pretty all right in the roll of a jaded Manhattanite whose charmed by Tom Hank's boyish character, although I think today's moviegoer sees a weird, pedophilic undertone in the romantic storyline. Others probably find the entire thing saccharine and unsatisfying.

Marshall moralizes: "Be careful what you wish for, or you might grow up to be a dick with a jaded girlfriend." Pretty basic.

The misfortune of "Big" is that it actually raises some primal, mythic questions without daring to really answer them, and so every time I see the little boy wishing to be big I wish the concept had first occurred to a better director.

Martin Scorsese was doing some great work at the time. Francis Ford Coppola could have made "Big" a huge comeback project.

Or even Peter Jackson would do. He was years away from viability as a director, but I think he would immediately notice that the boy never specified how big he wanted to be, so he'd just grow a few yards per day, and it would be a sort of remake of "The Amazing Colossal Man," except in this version the boy would scale the Empire State Building and have a fight with a squadron of attack planes.

Brian DePalma would concentrate on the story's strong

themes of sexuality, pointing out that while the boy wants only the stature of a man, he also inherits the urges of a man, and so he has to find ways to satisfy his newfound appetites. The man explores all the debauched delights New York City can offer a naive 30-year-old, but he ends up killing a hooker and obliterates his innocence. When he wishes himself back to normal, he realizes that he has been transformed from a boy in a man's body to a man in a boy's body. Like Dorian Gray, he has the face of a cherub, but his inward portrait is wicked and depraved.

In Coppola's version, the man recruits his school pals into a private army to do his bidding. One by one they hunt down and eliminate the crime bosses of New York in grisly but juvenile fashion. One mobster is bludgeoned to death by a forest of junior-sized hockey sticks. Another goes down in an astounding hail of BB-gun fire at a toll booth. The man-boy impales the butchered corpses of his victims on sharpened poles outside his headquarters. The CIA sends Martin Sheen on a Navy patrol boat up the East River to terminate the man-boy--terminate, with extreme prejudice.

However, Martin Scorsese's "Big" is the most riveting. It begins as the little boy is returning home from the carnival. We see that he's troubled, but there's no explanation. We are not shown the boy's wish or the genie. That's important. All we know is that he comes home sad and, in the morning, the boy is gone, and a disoriented, shirtless man is wandering around in his bedroom.

In Scorsese's version, the meeting of the man and his mother is gripping. As in the Marshall film, the mother's (and the viewers') first reaction is terror. She doesn't know the man is her son, so she begs him not to hurt her. He tries to clarify the situation, but she's too freaked out to understand. In the Scorsese film, when the man tries to identify himself, it confuses both the mother and the viewer. Who is this guy? Where's the kid?

The man manages to get his hands on his mother, but she flails away and smashes into a china hutch, where she splits her lip. The man sees his mother blood-splattered and bleeding, and now he panics, too. He cowers as his mother bombards him with books and potted plants, anything she can get her hands on. She doesn't seem to hear his babbling evidence—birthdays, scout troop numbers, the names of relatives. A cookie jar disintegrates on the man's brow and now he's bleeding, too. There's blood everywhere. At last the man thinks of one piece of irrefutable proof—the birthmark on his backside. He turns his back to her and pulls down the sweat pants he stole from her room because his pajamas are now too small for him, but the mother sees only the sweat pants she recognizes as her own, and the cartoon underwear she knows are her son's.

Until then, the mother assumed the man was a rapist or robber. When she sees the underwear, however, she realizes he has done something terrible with her son, who she thought was safe at school. Now she's the mother grizzly. She grabs a kitchen knife. The boy backs away but she's on him, slashing and stabbing, demanding to know what he's done with her son. The gash on the man's head is bleeding into his eyes. He squints and backs away, trying to avoid the mother as she frantically swings the knife. The man is also unaccustomed to his big feet, and he trips over an ottoman as his mother charges. She follows him to the floor, and the knife sinks into his chest.

A pool of blood widens on the carpet beneath the man. As his life slips away, the man gazes into his mother's eyes with a significance the mother and the viewer cannot help but notice. We don't know what it means because we don't know who the man is, and neither does the mother. She scrambles away from him, her mind racing to know how she'll recover her son now that his assailant lies dead in the living room.

Remember that the Scorsese interpretation takes place in a wished-for reality in which Marshall's film does not exist. We know very little to this point. And so we rightly assume that the boy is still out there, somewhere. The only unknown is whether he's alive or dead, and neither possibility seems more plausible than the other.

The mystery is probed by three independent investigations—one by a police detective, a second by the boy's best friend, and a third by the mother. The detective focuses on forensic evidence, and he finds that, oddly, the assailant's fingerprints are everywhere in the house, as though the man had been living in there for some time. This sheds doubt on the mother's assertion that she had not seen the man before the boy's disappearance. The detective even expresses interest in her as a murder suspect rather than the victim of a home invasion and possibly kidnapping.

The best friend's investigation takes place in the world of children. The neighborhood kids tell him things they withheld from the police and adults. But only the best friend also knows that the boy wanted to be bigger.

The mother makes her own discoveries. For example, while the detective has concluded the boy's ripped pajamas were torn from his body that morning, the mother notices that, unlikely as it may seem, it looks more like the boy had somehow outgrown the pajamas.

But more than anything else, she's troubled by the enigmatic expression on the man's face as he died. What was that expression? Was it regret? Was it pity?

The three sleuth on in isolation, their investigations intercut by flashbacks to the boy's final hours. The seaside carnival, the Ferris wheel, the girl, the genie. Eventually, the boy, mother, and detective are drawn together. They compare notes, reluctantly at first, suspiciously, but they realize that their findings overlap. They've reached some of the same conclusions.

Like three people solving a crossword together, they advance quickly after they join forces, but only the detective has the intellectual flexibility to face the utterly incredible conclusion, one that none of the viewers has even considered: the victim was the attacker, the attacker was the victim. Everyone in the film and everyone in the theater is tense with the query: how can this be?

With his nagging, irascible hunch and his police prerogatives, the detective locates the mechanized genie in the arcade game.

Flashback to the boy making his final wish.

The detective produces the tiny card the genie gave the boy, the one he found in the boy's bedroom on the morning the incident was reported.

The card reads, *Your wish is granted.*

The detective realizes the genie animates and dispenses wishes without the benefit of a power source: the genie is unplugged from any electrical outlet. He's beginning to believe the impossible is the only possible answer.

Before this, the detective was trying to determine if the man was a murder suspect or perhaps an accomplice, and so DNA and fingerprints from the boy had never been directly compared to that of the man. Now, however, he speeds to the lab with two samples.

"Just need to know how these two are related, if at all," he tells the technician in an effort to blind his experiment.

"Sure," says the technician. "No problem."

When the results come in, he phones the mother.

This alternate version would require some casting changes. Fans of Tom Hanks would argue that he possesses the necessary emotive range to play the man in Scorsese's film. I would strongly disagree, but that does not matter—Hanks would no longer be alive, because my wish would stipulate that he had drown during the filming of the movie "Splash," directed by Ron Howard, who would also drown in that same mishap. Thus, every movie Ron Howard film made after 1984 would not exist, and that includes "The DaVinci Code."

You are welcome.

Critics would label Scorsese's version of "Big" with phrases like "taut, mind-bending thriller," but it would actually be a straight tragedy. In Scorsese's version, the man is an unwilling Christ, atoning for the sin he himself commits. His mother is both Mary and Medea. Scorsese would defer to the scales of cosmic justice, unlike Marshall, who allows the boy to simply wish himself back to a happy ending, thereby breaking a cardinal rule of mythology: one cannot escape an ill-conceived wish.

Midas could not abdicate his golden touch. Semele could not take back her wish to see Zeus in his glory, even though Zeus knew very well that the sight of him would incinerate her.

The wheels of tragedy turn on the axle of a wish so pernicious—a wish not only to defer childhood, but to surrender it. Once granted, such a wish must end in doom. And of all the things to wish for—not riches, not immortality. Being big is something only a child would wish for, and this sharpens the tragedy.

As the mother answers the phone and receives the news from the detective, the void in the living room carpet where the huge blood stain has been removed takes on terrible significance.

She kneels where the man died, reliving the confrontation. From her memory, she pieces together the crazy things he said that morning and realizes that they were at times familiar, or that they made a weird kind of sense.

No, she thinks. The crazy things he said were true.

Was his face so utterly foreign? Did he not resemble his father?

He did.

Flashback to the crushing palindrome of the mother's story arc: she killed her son to save her son from being killed. Flashback to that moment, but now it's a boy lying on the floor, not a man. It's a little kid's life soaking into the carpeting, the knife jutting from his puny chest. She's thinking of that look he gave her. Every dying man and boy wishes for only one thing: not to be made well or to be big or anything else. Every dying man and boy wishes only to look on the face of his mother, and this is apparently true even if it is she who kills him.

Close-up of the man's pallid face as he stares up at her—same shot as in the opening scene.

Only now she understands.

And we understand.

It was love.

This story, like every other story, was about love. The look he gave her was love and the contentment of a wish fulfilled.

PAPER TIGERS
Amanda Luzzader

After we exchange the typical pleasantries about the weather and weekend plans, he says: "Picking up where we left off last time, tell me about a memory you have of a time when you were afraid when perhaps you didn't need to be," he says. "If you're comfortable doing that. Just any memory."

I think about it for a while. He waits.

"I have a memory of when I was little," I said. "I was four or five years old, I guess. One of my earliest memories."

He nods.

"It was Easter, and my family went to an Easter egg hunt at a park. It was for little kids, you know, toddlers and kindergartners. They put us all in a line at the edge of this big grassy area and there were plastic eggs and candy just everywhere. In the grass, around the trees. Hundreds. Thousands, maybe. Not really an Easter egg 'hunt,' I guess. More like an Easter egg gathering. My mom brought me to the line and gave me a little Easter basket and I stood there with all these other kids, looking at the eggs. I couldn't wait to get them, to put them in my basket."

"But you couldn't?"

"Well, somebody blew a whistle and all the kids lunged

forward into the grass and they started gathering up the eggs. Like the line just went forward and picked the grass clean. Some of the kids ran out in front. But not me. I was too afraid."

"Do you remember what specifically you were afraid of?"

"I don't know. The other kids, the noise and movement. I was scared of getting too far away from my mother. There was a guy in an Easter bunny costume—I was terrified of that. Other kids had completely full baskets within a minute or two. I just stood there on the starting line while my mom pushed me forward. My dad came over. They tried to talk me into getting out there. I just stood there. Pretty soon all of the eggs were gone. Every single one."

My therapist, Dr. Jim, leans back in his chair. He's an older man with a white beard and a friendly face.

"People with anxiety don't differentiate between the possible and the probable," he says. "They treat them both the same. So that every possible threat must be processed and reacted to as if it were probable. Or even inevitable."

That sounds like me.

"There are tigers and paper tigers," he says. "Threats that are probable and threats that are merely possible. People without anxiety can usually tell the difference without really trying too hard. The other kids in your memory—they processed very quickly and naturally that there was no danger in the crowds of people or the man dressed up like a rabbit."

I nod my head.

"But people with anxiety have to work extra hard to tell the difference between the paper tigers and real ones. And sometimes they're so wrapped up in processing false threats as real, they don't have the capacity do make the distinction. It doesn't occur to them to sort one from another."

This all makes perfect sense when I'm sitting in his office. But in normal life, all I see are things that make me afraid.

"What are some of the things that scare you now?"

"Getting attacked or murdered. Getting raped. Kidnapped."

"And how do these fears manifest themselves in your daily life, your behavior?"

"I don't go out at night. Once it's dark, I lock the doors and I don't go out at night."

"You know that kidnappings and rapes don't happen very often, right? And murders?"

"One in 18,000 people in America will be killed this year."

"Okay," says Dr. Jim, "but this is not Detroit. This is not Chicago. The odds are much lower here. You know this, right?"

"Landerton was named the safest town in America last year."

"That's right," says Dr. Jim. "You see my point? Getting murdered is possible, but it's not probable. So, there's no need to hide as soon as it's dark. It doesn't help."

"Can't hurt."

Dr. Jim smiles patiently.

"No, I see your point," I say. "It's just that it's—"

"—not that easy," he says. "No. It's not."

"So, what can I do?"

He tells me about several strategies. One is to restate my fear using a Donald Duck voice.

"I'm thow afwaid!" cries Dr. Jim in a very exuberant but passable imitation of Donald Duck. "Dat man ith wathing me! He'th gonna git me!"

I laugh at him.

"See? It disarms the threat. It makes a mockery of it. And it can give you a moment or two to respond more reasonably. You try."

"What, now? Here?"

"Sure. Just repeat a scary thought or idea using a silly voice."

"I don't know how to talk that way."

"Doesn't have to be Donald Duck. Try a baby voice or a Valley Girl. Anything."

I try SpongeBob SquarePants. "Oh no! It's getting daaark! I better lock all my—" but I can't finish it, because I start laughing again.

Dr. Jim grins. "See?"

"Yeah," I say. "Yeah. I like that."

About a week later I'm at the library. I've finished up a little research. I'm actually majoring in psychology, so I'm not only a mental health patient, I'm a student of it. I've just finished the bibliography of my term paper on chronic post-trauma effects on financially disadvantaged young people, but I'm hanging out in the lobby on the main floor, pretending to read a book.

Pretending, but I'm really just watching Scarf Boy.

(That's not his real name.)

I don't know his name because I've never had the guts to ask. He works at the circulation desk. I call him Scarf Boy because he always wears a scarf. Not like a winter scarf, but a fashionable scarf. He wears cool jackets, too, especially now that it's getting cooler. His whole look is on point. He knows when to wear ankle boots and when to wear sneakers. He uses lots of layers. He wears hats sometimes but not all the time. He looks like he stepped out of a cologne ad in Cosmo.

"What's your major? Where do you live? Where are you from?" Those are the questions I know he'll ask me if we ever get into a conversation, and those are the questions I know I'll trip over and get wrapped up in and make a fool of myself over. I despise small-talk. I just want to cut right to the relaxed, witty conversations.

So, for now, I always have a book to read in the lobby by the circulation desk. But it's a Saturday, and there's hardly anyone in the library, and so I wonder if Scarf Boy will catch me staring at him over the top of my book and think I'm a dork. Or that he'll be creeped out by me.

There I go. Over-thinking, over-worrying. My heart rate is up. Take a breath. Talk like Spongebob.

I can't do it aloud, but I think of the voice in my head: "Oooh, no! Scarf Boy won't liiiiike you if he catches you looking!"

Wow. That helps. I relax (a little—I never relax completely). I read a sentence in the book then look. Read, then look.

He's really cute.

"The library will be closing in 15 minutes," says a voice over a PA. "Please bring your selections to the circulation desk."

Fortunately, I always make sure I have something to return and something to check out, too, so I can at least pretend I might talk to Scarf Boy one of these days as I leave to go home.

There's a book return box just down the counter from where Scarf Boy is working, but I give him the book I checked out last week. I give it right to him, and then give him the book I'm checking out. I won't read it, of course. I wonder if I should feel bad for the person who might hypothetically want to read the books I check out and never even open.

Scarf Boy smiles as I approach. Such a great smile. Sandy blond hair that falls below his brow and shades his blue eyes. I haven't seen this scarf. It's gray with a hounds tooth check and a big lining of frill. Goes great with that shirt, I think. This guy can blend grays and earth tones. He's sublime.

Scarf boy asks, "Find everything you were looking for?"

"Fine, thanks," I reply.

Scarf Boy laughs.

Oy. He scans the book. I grab it race for the door.

"Come again soon," he says with kindly chuckle.

"You too!" I say as I plunge through the exit.

Double oy.

It's dark outside.

And cold. It's fall. I guess I'm not quite used to it getting dark so early. I should have been home an hour ago. It's a ten-minute walk to the car and it's dark. As Dr. Jim will tell you, another student would not have to think twice about a ten-minute walk through what can only be called one of the safest college campuses in the world.

But they're not me.

Okay, I think. Paper tigers.

My boots seem to clamor and clack on the sidewalk as I go.

I imagine eyes upon me. The eyes of someone with ill-intent. Ten minutes. I walk a little faster.

On the campus there are lights literally everywhere. On every corner, on every wall of every building. And there are "rape phones." They call them "emergency phones," but we all know they're for rape. Probably one reason this campus has been deemed so safe. In the dark, in the night, I see them glowing—a little blue light at every rape phone. I see at least three from where I am. Most of them are really far away, but there's one up ahead of me. Paper tigers. I'm fine. Really. In ten minutes I'll be within sprinting distance of at least one rape phone, maybe two.

Even so, I'm breathing hard. The campus lights really are everywhere, but unfortunately they're tasteful and down-pointing, and there are dark gaps between them, gulfs that must be crossed, dark voids that surely harbor shadowed people ready to do me harm.

Paper tigers.

I hear something behind me. Not loud, but rhythmic. They're footsteps. Not close, but stealthy. I wheel around, looking for the source of the sound. I'm bad at doing that. I can never tell where sounds are coming from. There are buildings all around, and the sound ricochets, deceiving my senses.

Is it behind me? I think so. I turn around and in the dark place between two pools of light emitting from the tasteful, environmentally friendly, down-facing light fixtures, I catch a flitting movement.

Someone's running my way.

Well, not exactly. I'm heading across campus on the main quad sidewalk, and someone is loping along a nearby sidewalk, one that attaches to the quad walk a little ways ahead of me. I turn around and go the other way.

What was it that Dr. Jim said to do about paper tigers? I don't recall. Something about cartoons or Donald Duck. Talk like Donald Duck. Talk like Spongebob Squarepants. How could that possibly help me?

I feel the tears coming. I run.

As I look back, I almost trip and fall, but I see the runner. It's man. A large man. He has reached the quad walk and he has turned onto the quad sidewalk and he is now running directly toward me from behind. His footfalls are furtive and soft but each one seems to deafen me. I don't know how far behind he is. I'm so bad with distances.

Talk like Spongebob.

This is not Detroit.

Paper tiger.

My face is wet from crying.

I look back, almost stumble again. The man wears a black hoodie with the hood up. I can't see his face. I sprint between the tasteful light fixtures and their environmentally friendly, downward-facing shades and the pools of light beneath them. I run as fast as I can.

The large man is faster. His footfalls are right behind me. I think I let out a yelp, I turn to see where he is and my foot lands on the grass and the uneven surface puts me off balance and this time I really stumble and I'm sort of flailing in the grass when the large man in the dark hoodie passes by me.

He gives me a quizzical look and says, "Y'alright?"

I say, "Yes, I'm okay!"

(In Spongebob's voice.)

The man runs on and is lost in the darkness.

The spaces between the lights are as black as ever now and I know the jogger was just a jogger—a paper jogger so to speak—but there is darkness all around me.

Where am I?

I'm somewhere in that weird area between the main parking terrace and the new engineering building construction site and a block of student housing. Where was I going? My car.

Where is my car? Paper tigers.

I'm turned around at this point so instead of turning back toward my car, I somehow head back toward the library and I walk that direction until I actually see the library.

The library is dark now. The library is closed. Because it's late now. Because it's the weekend. Because it's dark. I should be home. Talk like a duck.

I'm at the library, which is ten minutes from my car. I turn around. Again. I start to cry. Again. I can't breathe.

At the crosswalk I crossed just ten minutes earlier, I pause instinctively, but only for a split-second, and then I cross.

And a car nearly runs me down.

There's a deafening honk, the rough hiss of tires stopping short on asphalt, and the glare of very close headlamps.

I'm frozen in the crosswalk. I don't know what to do. Can't remember what you're supposed to do when someone almost hits you with a car. I stand there with my hands out, like that would have helped if the car would've hit me.

The car's window comes down and a head emerges. I squint. Sandy blond hair. Is that a gray scarf with hounds tooth patterning?

"Scarf Boy?" I say.

His brow furrows, but he says, "Hi! Weren't you just inside?" He gestures toward the library with a nod of his head.

"Yeah," I say. "I was. I needed a book."

Paper tigers.

"Also, I think your scarf is great. Really ties the outfit together. Grays and earth tones. Well done."

He laughs. "Thanks. Thanks for noticing. But, uhm, where are you going, and why aren't you there already? Didn't you leave like twenty minutes ago?"

I'm mortified. I'm terrified. Screw Dr. Jim and his paper tigers. I will never go out after dark again.

"Could I give you a ride home?" asks Scarf Boy.

This isn't how I imagined getting to know Scarf Boy. I imagined espresso, and avocado toast, and a witty, relaxed conversation.

"Could you? Please?"

He laughs again. "Get in."

I get into his little car, averting my face as much as I can so that he won't be able to tell I've been crying. I don't think this works.

"You okay? You in trouble?"

"I don't know," I say. "I don't like being out this late."

"It's barely past nine," he says.

"I know, right? I should've been home an hour ago."

"So, where can I take you?"

"Oh. The D Lot. Please."

"That's not far. Just right over here, right?"

"Yeah. Thanks."

I look over at him. So what if he can tell if I've been crying. He looks over and smiles. Then I see it. His scarf as fallen away from his neck and I see it—climbing up his neck and out of his shirt collar is a tattoo. I blink a few times to clear my vision, to make sure I'm seeing what I think I'm seeing. Then I realize the D Lot is coming up on our right.

"I'm in this lot," I tell him. "Here. D Lot."

"I know," says Scarf Boy. "That's not where we're going."

He keeps driving. We pass by the D Lot.

I look back over at him, at the tattoo.

It's a tiger.

And his blue eyes look dark now. And suddenly a Henry Kissinger quote comes to mind. One I'd heard a long time ago and forgotten. "Even a paranoid can have enemies." I thought then of the fear I'd felt my whole life, my anxiety. And as he accelerates down the road I know, without a doubt, I'd been right to have been afraid.

THE BLANKET
Chadd VanZanten

My sniffles turned into a cold, the cold turned to the flu, and then this flu took things a few steps further, like a guy who wants to fight you at the supermarket because he thinks you got in line in front of him. The flu went ahead and mutated into some kind of wracking, soul-devouring plague.

I really try not to miss too much work. If I'm just a little sick, I'll go into the office and shut the door with a sign that says *SICK! STAY OUT.* Or I'll go in after hours. If all else fails I work from home. But this thing sank deep into my tissues, broke my will. I felt like I was transforming into some other life form. It was time to admit defeat, and so I hit the couch, wrapped in an enormous blanket.

Let me tell you about this blanket. It was gigantic and very heavy. I don't remember the exact dimensions of the original, but it could smother a king-sized bed and wrinkle up on the floor all the way around.

This really old woman from my neighborhood made it for me when I was just a little kid. She took a liking to me one summer when I helped her pick the raspberries that grew alongside her house. I don't remember her name. Daniels, I think. She was tall and gangling, with narrow shoulders and wide hips. She had a wispy white beard, and her nose was the shape of a flattened lemon. With her bowed legs and long forearms, I sometimes thought she looked like an orangutan in a house dress.

I came home from school one day to find the blanket in the middle of my bedroom.

"What's this?" I asked my mother.

It resembled a blanket or bedding of some kind, but the blankets I used on my bed were just that--blankets. A thin layer of soft, fleecy material with cartoon characters or football helmets all over it. The blanket my parents used on their bed was light and satiny and stuffed with feathers. This thing in my bedroom had been folded into a squarish heap four feet across, and still it was as high as my navel. It was heavy, substantial. It looked like a entire bed folded into fourths.

"Mrs. Daniels made it for you," said my mother. "She wanted to thank you for helping her pick the raspberries. It's a quilt."

"A what?" I asked, touching it lightly with my fingertips.

"It's a quilt. See? It's quilted with stuffing inside. A lot of stuffing. I bet it'll keep you very warm."

Quilt, quilted—these were new words to me. My mother had never bought a quilt, much less made one.

"But what's it for?" I asked. Surely it was a protective cover for the car. Or maybe the boat.

"Sweetie," said my mom. "It's a big, homemade blanket."

The cheap flannel on top of the blanket was a vomit-colored gray-brown, printed with tiny wildflowers that from a short distance looked like giant blue and red fleas. The underside was a flannel of a fuzzier kind, electric sky blue in color. The yarn tie-offs were burnt orange. It is to this day the ugliest article of textile craft I've ever seen.

But I grew to love the blanket, and it could keep you warm--if you could keep it from suffocating you. I often wondered how the Widow Daniels ever got it to our house. She lived several blocks away. I later concluded that it had finished her off; she died that winter.

The blanket was never used on any bed. It was way too big. Instead, I mostly used it while sprawled on the floor watching TV or when I slept in the living room, like when my cousins stayed overnight. We'd spread it on the floor as a communal pallet. In the morning we propped kitchen chairs underneath to make a massive Bedouin tent.

Even when I was old enough to understand its ugliness and dis-utility, I continued to grow attached to the thing. I was like Charlie Brown's friend Linus, only my blanket was bigger than an airborne ranger's parachute. When I was a teenager, I'd settle in front of the TV on Friday nights, enwrapped in the ugly blanket like a Lakota Indian in a buffalo hide. On Saturday morning I would awaken to find myself swallowed as if by a huge caterpillar with an electric-blue stomach lining.

I took the blanket to college, and I hung onto it when I got married. My wife hated it. It was a frowsy, logistical nightmare. It took two people to fold it, for one thing, and you had to be really careful or you'd knock down a lamp or a picture on the wall. The blanket cupboard was far too small to store the blanket, so it sat in the bottom of the hall closet, and even there it had to be wedged in and wrestled out.

The biggest problem was that it was nearly too large even for the double-size industrial front-loading washers at the laundromat, and so it was infrequently laundered. This made my wife call it the "household germ and virus storage and retrieval system."

"It's dusty and gross and it's probably got smallpox in it," she said.

She was probably right. I often crawled under it when I was sick.

So, I lay there on the couch, simmering with some flavor of rabid influenza, just buried by this blanket, this expanse of stale-smelling and dusty fabric. I was trying to utilize the blanket as a sort of sensory-deprivation shroud, to hide from everything. My fever horribly exaggerated any movement or light or sound. It made me nauseous and jittery, so I was trying not to see, hear, or exist. In fact, I didn't even really want to sleep, either, knowing the fever would claw its way into my dreams, turn them against me. But not even the blanket could hide me from that.

I tend to get very high fevers when I'm sick, and they always give me the most sickening nightmares. To me, that's the worst part of getting sick. When I was only fifteen or sixteen, I got really bad stomach bug and my temperature went up to 103. The whole time, I kept dreaming I was in a biplane, attacking a creature that climbed to the top of the Empire State Building. It wasn't a giant ape, but a giant kitten, skeletal and elongated; its bony spine and each of its legs twenty yards long or more. It gripped the observation deck with its hind feet and reared up into the sky over Manhattan like an emaciated bear. Stretched over its bones was dry skin with patches of thin black fur. From its spine sprouted a pair of vast, leathery wings, with which it roiled buffets of turbulence that threatened to send my biplane into a stall. Its head was like that of a road-killed cat long dead—desiccated, eyeless.

My biplane had a machine gun, so I soared down out of the sun from 1,200 feet and pressed the gun paddle, releasing a stream of lead, but the kitten's body was so spindly that few rounds found their marks. The rest flew out over Stuyvesant, and I came low over the East Village. As I banked the biplane toward Queens, I saw people in taxi cabs on FDR Drive. Then I climbed, passing 1,000 feet, then 1,200, 1,500 feet. With the Queensboro Bridge under me, I snapped an Immelmann and looped back to midtown, diving for speed. This time I put the iron cross hairs on the kitten's papery wing skin and fired true, but the bullets flitted through, raining down on SoHo and Tribeca.

And so I hunched on the couch, bracing for a new onslaught of vivid, dream world awfulness. The blanket was wrapped around me and up over my head like a huge hood, with only vaguely tube-like construct around my face so that I could see out and breathe a little. As I peered out of the hood-tunnel, I noticed a large flap of the blanket had fallen onto the floor. Even though the blanket totally enveloped me like a tortilla wrapping around a burrito, some stray corner of it flapped to the floor, a flap so large that it crossed the living room and lapped at the legs of a chair in the dining room some eighteen feet away. That strange jittery jumpiness was creeping into my thoughts. My eyes drooped and snapped open, drooped and snapped awake again. Everything turned huge and infinitely small at the same moment, and a soft calamity of sound raged at the edge of my hearing.

I remained motionless. I tried to. It was the only thing I could do, the only thing that might hold back the visions. After a while I fell into a shallow doze, but then my wife woke me.

"This is getting out of hand," she snapped at me. "You've got to get rid of it."

My wife and I had been married long enough to use a lot of what they call nonverbal communication, based not in intimacy, but rather on a standing assumption that we will disagree about most things. Sometimes I thought our marriage was just a contest to see who was right the most often. She stood in the living room, hands on her hips, shaking her head testily as she surveyed the blanket as it sprawled out onto the floor.

My tongue and throat were dry, but from inside the blanket I croaked out a response that she correctly interpreted as a request for clarification about what it was she thought was getting out of hand, and she further understood my preemptive and presumptive denial that anything was, in fact, out of hand.

"This quilt," she said. "It's gotten big enough. I'm taking it to the dump. I'm sick of it."

Now I poked my head out of the blanket folds like some diseased rodent. I looked around, squinting. Reality wobbled and flickered. The blanket now covered the living room and hallway, draping everything in its vomitous brown wildflowers. It covered all the furniture, though my wife had evidently uncovered the house plants. The TV was under it somewhere, the audio dampened by the fabric and felt. I tried to act as if nothing was wrong.

"We are not throwing this blanket away." I rasped. "I love this blanket."

"We have other blankets," she said.

"I've had this blanket since I was a kid."

"We have newer ones. Nicer ones. Ones that don't smell funny. Ones that don't suddenly start growing."

"Blankets don't grow."

"Look around you, dear. This one grows. It's going to the dump."

"Oh, that's just great," I said. "Just one more thing where you call the shots, huh? What happened to consulting each other? Like we said. Hm? Talking things over? One blanket starts growing and suddenly my opinion doesn't mean anything around here."

She walked out.

"And besides," I shouted after here, "it's not growing."

It kept growing.

The next day, I heard a helicopter outside, and on the TV news I saw video from its camera. It was a shot of my house, showing the blanket spilling from the windows, the doors, the top of the chimney. The blanket covered some of the nearby houses. Emergency vehicles moved along the edges of the blanket, and police set up barricades to direct traffic to unobstructed roads.

Footage from the ground showed the blanket advancing with the menace of cooling lava. Broken water pipes, trees pushed down, fires. Someone took cell phone video of an old man with a walker who got engulfed by a section of the blanket as it spilled suddenly from the roof of Taco Bell.

"You see?" said my wife. "Even the news says it's growing. We have to do something."

"You do realize that I'm sick, right? This is as sick as I've ever been. Can you stop right-fighting for a day or two until I feel better? Is that too much to ask?"

I retreated into the now majestic flannel chrysalis. So much room there. Room to heal. Room to live apart. I began to create a system of tunnels, like the VC dug beneath Vietnam, with traps and blind alleys and sleeping chambers. I could now go anywhere in the house without removing myself from the blanket. There was no light inside, but I knew the way.

One day, a team of scientists came to my house. They had hiked in over the ridges and hills of the blanket that I heard now extended 90 miles in every direction. The scientists had backpacks and hiking poles. They asked me if I knew why my blanket kept growing. My wife was standing behind them with that look on her face--that "well, are you ready to admit who's right" look on her face.

"Don't be ridiculous," I said.

They produced an environmental impact study that predicted the blanket was impairing regional agriculture would soon threaten the habitat of sensitive and endangered animal and plant species.

"As you can see," said one, referring to the charts and data, "local fruit growers have been wiped out for the season."

My wife threw her hands in the air. "The whole season!" she said.

"Okay," I conceded after she'd left the room in a huff. "It's grown a little, but you guys are exaggerating. I'm in this sort of spat with my wife, see. And it's complicated and I wonder if you guys could do me a solid and maybe fudge things so that I can save some face here. If she's right I am never going to hear the end of this."

The scientists looked at each other. Then one of them showed me photographs taken from space that clearly showed that the blanket now covered one tenth of the state.

It's not like I didn't believe them. The TV and Internet had stopped working a long time ago. The blanket had moved the house off its foundation and started to break it apart. Huge cracks and voids ran along every wall and ceiling. Soon the house simply collapsed and the pieces floated away on the flannel sea. An acrid, ashy smoke blew in on the wind from the outer edges of the blanket--the results, I presumed, of the havoc the blanket was wreaking as it advanced. I knew the scientists were right, but I could not let her be right. Not about this. Not about the blanket.

So when the scientists came back to gather more data, I told them all to go to hell. I stood and the blanket lifted me ten feet high, then twenty. I looked down on the barren, odd-looking landscape. No houses anymore. No trees. Just bland flannel fabric as far as the eye could see. A few dogs loped along a ridge line of blanket, chasing the pathetic birds and mammals who'd been unable to get beyond the blanket's borderlands.

I lifted myself higher, and the scientists scurried before me, fumbling their clipboards and hiking gear. I chased them and was met by phalanx of reporters who'd been camped on hillsides of blanket surrounding the site where my house had once been. They were all on extended assignment to cover the blanket's ground zero zone.

It was, of course, the only thing being reported on by the news. Around-the-clock, serial coverage in all the big papers and on all the news and media. There were big photos of the blanket, which was now suffocating millions of acres of the Earth's surface. Entire issues of Newsweek and other magazines were devoted to the matter. On the cover of National Geographic was me in my bathrobe, my face pale and stubbled, mouth gaping in a shout, and the large headline quoting me as screaming: *It's Not Growing.*

It kept growing.

Governments began to shut down. Cities and towns were completely wiped out. Economies collapsed. The climate changed.

I decided it was time for a family meeting. I thought maybe if we all came together, I could get ahead of the situation, maybe triangulate the truth of the matter so that my wife couldn't gloat.

"Honey? Kids? Get in here. Family meeting time."

I stalked around the labyrinthine tunnels of the blanket for several days looking for them, but they were nowhere to be found. The system of tunnels sprawled to infinite complexity, stretching thousands of miles with caverns of staggering size. I looked and looked.

"Kids! I mean right now! Family meeting. If everyone doesn't meet me right now where New Mexico used to be, there is going to be trouble in this household!"

But they were gone. Fled or taken away--or worse. I heard (and felt) the rumble and thump of distant artillery fire from the far-off perimeters of the blanket. The world was at war with the blanket.

I did not know who was winning, but I suspected it was me.

Life on earth eventually slowed to a crawl.

One day, after many years, I was investigating "the Leading Edge," as the earth's few survivor's called it, the edge of the blanket, that was still advancing, only an inch or so per day, into the last uncovered areas. There were still a few places on earth it had not reached. I wasn't sure where it was, what place it had once been, but it looked like a tundra that had been blackened by warfare before the armies of earth had been conquered. Out there on the nearly featureless and wasted landscape, I saw a small campfire burning. The blanket carried me over to it.

It was my wife.

"Fran? What are you doing here?" I said.

She had aged. Although the blanket had only been growing for a few years, Fran looked as though she'd aged ten hard years. Her face was drawn with misery. She was thin and sickly. I guess I should have expected that. There was no food or clean water. She huddled over the small cook fire, boiling what looked like lentils. Nearby was our old four-person Coleman tent, tattered now, and very faded. There was a backpack and what looked like a few provisions.

"Come inside," I said. "I've got food, and it's so cold out here. Come inside."

She scoffed. "Never. Look at what you've done."

"Look at what?" I asked. "I've got the flu. I wanted to stay home and wrap up in my favorite blanket. Another week or so and I'll be good as new. God, why do you have to criticize everything I do? Why are you always trying to get rid of my stuff?"

"Why do you have to be so stubborn? This is all your doing. Even when the earth is dead and entombed, you can't admit when you're wrong."

"What do you want?" I said. "Why are you hanging around here?"

"I want to see if the children would come out."

"They're never coming out," I sneered. "They wanted to stay with me."

"You see? You see how thoughtless you are? You don't even know where they are!"

The blanket surged seeming to rise up to meet her anger and browbeating. Maybe it was my anger surging through it. In any case the blanket gathered itself like a wave and surged forward with shocking fury like a great hand swatting a fly on a table. I should say that the blanket was no longer just the one layer of quilted material. There were multiple, numerous laminates, and it was hard and heavy like the skin of a whale. Its cross section may have been 25 feet thick out there on that scorched tundra. It was like a garbage truck or Zamboni had driven over my wife. When the blanket withdrew, Fran had been reduced to a smear of crushed and disarticulated bones and flesh, suspended in a kind of thick slurry of blood and fluids that immediately began soaking into the ground.

There may have been survivors, people and creatures who adapted to life above or beneath the covers. I never did find the kids. Eventually it was just the dead rock of the world and me, wrapped together in the mighty blanket, rolling endlessly through the solar system.

To me, the blanket never changed. It looked and smelled the same as it always did when I snuggled down to sleep at night. Sometimes I poked my head out to look out over the endless knots of the quilted surface stretching to the horizon in all directions. Sometimes I thought about visiting sections of blanket that covered very distant parts of the world, but I never got around to it.

At night, the cold dead stars shown down on me, and I stayed in the blanket forever.

IF SOMEONE WANTS IN
Amanda Luzzader

Donna's house is across the street from mine. While the baby naps, I stand on the sidewalk in front my house and study her front door, windows, garage. The houses on this street are all very similar. I'm wondering what made her home the target. Things like that aren't supposed to happen in this little neighborhood.

Mindy from next door comes out and joins me on the sidewalk.

"Guess you heard," Mindy says.

I nod.

"Hope they catch the creep," she says.

"She woke up and he was just there, I guess."

"Yeah," says Mindy. "Got in through a window."

"Oh, I heard he came in through the garage."

Mindy shrugs. "Amelia said he jimmied a window."

"What does that mean? 'Jimmied'?"

She shrugs. "They know ways to get in."

"We're getting an alarm system," I tell her. "I'm locking every deadbolt each night and keeping all the outside lights on."

Mindy shrugs. "If someone wants in bad enough, alarms

and locked doors won't stop 'em."

I look over my shoulder at my own house. When we bought it, I loved the numerous windows that let light in.

"Gotta pick up the kids," says Mindy. "See you later."

It gets windy as the sun goes down. Mindy's words echo in my mind—what she said about someone wanting to get in. I check and double-check the locks on the doors and windows. I turn on all the outside lights. Just before it gets dark, I go to my bedroom window and look carefully at the lock. It's aluminum and spring-loaded somehow, and it grips the inside of the window frame. How could it be unlocked from outside, I wonder. It seems impossible. But these prowlers, these rapists, they know how to get in even if it's not obvious to me. They could just break the glass, I guess.

My phone rings and I practically jump out of my PJs.

It's Brad, checking in on us. I tell him the baby isn't tired, so we're going to play or read a book.

"Then we'll go to bed," I say.

"Did you lock the back door?" asks Brad.

"Yeah."

"And the other doors?"

"Uh huh."

"The windows?"

"Yes. Everything."

"Good. Then I think you'll be okay, babe. You're safe."

I don't say anything for a while.

"You okay?" he asks.

Out in the kitchen my dinner sits cold and untouched on the kitchen table. I want to tell Brad he needs to come home now—forget Atlanta, forget the sales conference. Come home.

"I'm fine," I say. "Have a good time."

"Don't worry, babe," he says. "Go to bed. I'll see you tomorrow."

"Okay. Bye."

"Night, babe."

I keep the phone to my ear. Brad doesn't hang up.

After a few seconds he says, "Babe?"

"Yeah."

"Don't call the cops," he says quietly. "Okay?"

He's trying to be nice, but it stings. A few months ago I called the police while Brad was gone. I thought there was someone in the garage. The police came but didn't find anyone. After what happened at Donna's house, I think there really might have been someone out there. The officer said everything was locked up and undisturbed, but I couldn't sleep for the next two nights, and Brad had to come home from his work trip a day early. He was annoyed.

"Okay?" Brad repeats.

The wind buffets the windows, hisses in the treetops outside.

"But—Donna," I say.

"We don't know everything that happened at Donna's," he says in a quiet but firm voice. "Nobody's said anything. Shawn said he heard it was her own brother. Said he was on drugs and broke in to steal stuff and get money."

"We need an alarm system," I say.

"No, babe," says Brad. "Everything's okay. You're safe. Go to bed. You can call me if you get scared."

I stare at the window lock.

"Okay?" says Brad.

"Okay."

"I gotta go," he says. "I'll see you tomorrow. I love you."

I keep the phone to my ear until he hangs up. Then I put it back into the pocket of my PJs and look down at my cooing baby. It'll be a while before he'll sleep. We go downstairs and sit on the floor to play. But my eyes keep wandering to my mantle clock. Its loud tick-tock makes me think of a time-bomb. I turn on the TV and flip aimlessly through the stations. News. Infomercial. Golf. Black-and-white movie. News. In the half-second of silence between each station, I hear a noise. I hear something in the house. Or outside. Or something outside that wants to get in.

I mute the TV, but I can't mute the baby. He seems to think the lowered volume on the TV signals increased volume from him. He chatters and babbles, which is usually adorable to me, but now it's frustrating. I close my eyes and tilt my head.

Is it the cat? The furnace? A mouse?

It's a cross between a tapping and a scratching.

There's an urban legend about a young couple whose car breaks down along some remote country lane in the middle of the night. The boy goes to get help, leaving the girl alone. She locks the doors and falls asleep, but wakes suddenly to the sound of a strange, soft sound. Something is tapping or scraping the roof of the car. Or touching. It's a soft sound. Too terrified to open the door to get out of the car, or even to open a window and peek out, the girl huddles down in the seat. The soft tapping-touching sound goes on and on. Finally, a policeman comes and bangs on the window. He seems shocked to have found her. She's panic-stricken, almost insensible. The cop convinces her to open the door, but before he coaxes her out, he says, "I'm gonna take you to my cruiser now. It's right over there. But I want you to do something for me. Whatever you do, I want you to stay with me and don't look back at your car. She agrees and steps out of the car, and the cop leads her toward his police cruiser. "Don't look back there," he repeats. But she can't help it. She turns to look and there is the boy, dead and suspended above the car by his feet from a massive tree. As the wind moves the tree branches, the boy's fingers drag across the roof of the car.

That's exactly what this sounds like.

If I'm going to sleep at all, I'll have to know what's making the noise. It seems to be coming from a spare bedroom down the hall. My baby smiles as I scoop him into my arms. I flip on every light switch I pass as I make my way down the hall. My steps are slow and careful and catlike.

The door groans a little as it opens. Staying back in the hall, I grope inside for the light switch. The room is unused and mostly empty. We haven't really fixed it up yet and the light inside is gloomy—just a couple low-wattage bulbs. It's colder in there, too—the heater vents are shut. I hoist the baby higher on my hip and step inside to listen.

The sound is coming from the window.

Swallowing hard, I hold the baby tighter and take a few steps toward the window. When I'm within arm's length, I reach out and with my index finger extended, I raise a single louver of the blinds. I squint and peer through the crack, but I see nothing but a sliver of blackness. The blinds rattle as I grab them by the corner and lift them a little. But it's too dark to see outside and the blinds twist and sag awkwardly as I try to move them and hold the baby at the same time. I lean forward, afraid even to breath. I notice all at once that the noise has stopped. I stare out the window.

And then I see another set of eyes returning my gaze.

I gasp hoarsely and stagger back to the door, almost dropping the baby in the process. The blinds rattle down into place.

My hand darts into the pocket of my PJs and the phone is in my hand. I'm going to do it. I'm calling the police. I'll run to Mindy's and call 9-1-1. Screw you, Brad. You're not here alone. You're not here in the dark with a tiny baby.

But everything had happened so fast. Was it really eyes I'd seen? Eyes in the darkness looking almost calmly up at me from out there in the junipers?

"There's just nothing out there, Ms. Davidson," the officer had said as he came into the house from the garage again.

"You looked under the van?" I'd said.

"I did." He nodded emphatically. "And Officer Alvarez is double-checking the backyard."

"You didn't see anything?"

"The garage door is secure. Windows shut. Nothing's out of place."

I nodded reluctantly.

Officer Alvarez came in. "All clear," he said.

"Seems like a false alarm this time. Feel free to call us if you have any more trouble."

But don't call, is what his tone told me.

I put the phone back in my pocket. I have to check the

window again. Then I'll call. Then I'll run.

The few steps back to the window feel like walking through mud. I exhale forcefully. My hand is trembling. I grab the pull string on the blinds and yank it down. The blinds retract up the valence with a cacophonous metallic scrape.

A pair of eyes. Livid face. Bald head. Manic grin.

I startle back violently and I let out a bellowing scream. My hand clutches the pull string of the blind. I can't seem to let it go. Not until I get too far away, and almost tear away the entire window treatment, do I release it, and the blinds cascade noisily down.

I lean heavily into the wall and grip the baby. He squirms and complains. I'd only gotten another split-second glimpse, but it was long enough. My throat seems to constrict. It's like breathing through a coffee straw. I grip the baby with one hand and fumble for my phone with the other. I'd seen a face, and he'd seen me. Which means he's not just a peeping tom or burglar.

Is he toying with me? Does he want to get in? Can anything stop him?

But my mind spins back to something. Then it spins back again, spins back to something important, something significant.

I try to swallow but my throat is so dry and tight. I feel as though something has frozen me in place. It's not just flight or fight, you know. That's a nice, rhymey way to sum up the effects of surging adrenaline, but there's one more that nobody mentions—freeze. It's flight or fight or freeze. Some creatures freeze to defend themselves. To hide or blend in. I can't move. I'm frozen. I bring out my phone and tap the screen. My hands are so shaky. The baby squirms.

My thumb almost touches down on the *Emergency Call* button.

No. Wait. Not yet. Think. There's something I'm not thinking through. I just need to think this through. And then, somewhere in my mind, I feel something or hear something or see something. It's like snapping a puzzle piece into place.

That smile.

I hoist the baby onto my hip and go to the window once more. I take the pull string and yank it again. The blinds slide up noisily and compress together, and I secure the string so they won't fall shut.

There in the window, with the darkness outside and the light at my back, I see the soft, shadowy reflection of my baby's face. He sees my face in our reflection and smiles at me. Those eyes, that pale face, little bald head, crazy toothless grin.

I kiss him on top of his hairless head and smile sheepishly at our own reflections.

The soft tapping, touching sound? A branch brushing the window, maybe. Or the cat. Or nothing at all.

When I switch off the light, the blackness in the room matches the blackness outside. I turn and look through the window. It's a lovely night. The breeze blows the leaves of the trees and makes a gentle rushing sound like radio static. The stars glimmer through high clouds, and the lights of the neighbors' houses glow softly in the darkness.

THE BLACK GOD
Chadd VanZanten

After eight and a half years as lead sales rep at the Fitzgerald Group, Lawrence quit. The best job he ever had, the longest job he ever had, eight years--Lawrence up and quit.

To be clear, he didn't resign, didn't clean out his desk, or stop driving into work. He didn't quit eating lasagna in the executive lounge. He just quit doing his job.

At first it was just a lot of sitting in his office and playing on the Internet, but soon Lawrence sat at his desk reading books concealed behind manila file folders. Last quarter he read The Sum of All Fears, Cardinal of the Kremlin, and a book about making money in bear markets. If this quarter's projections are accurate, he'll get through The Shining, Carrie, the unabridged version of The Stand, and a book on day trading.

A big company like Fitzgerald runs itself. As time goes by longtime employees get noticed less and less, and not much happens when they give up. That's why no one said anything to Lawrence. That's why he wasn't fired right away. It'd be like finding a very slow leak in a very large rubber raft. You'd have to feel around so carefully, put your ear to the rubber, touch your hand along each seam. It'd take forever to find.

Sometimes it's easier just to pump it up again and keep going.

When Lawrence first took the job at Fitzgerald, Carrie walked him to the front door of their apartment every morning, no matter how early, and sent him off with his laptop and his briefcase and a kiss on the mouth. Trent was just eight years old back then, and Carrie told Lawrence that Trent would pretend to go to work just like Daddy. He pretended his lunch box was a briefcase.

Lawrence hustled around the office and he did things the older guys couldn't do, wouldn't do--using sales data and stats more effectively, spotting trends and gaps in their market coverage. Instead of taking days to collate and analyze a year's worth of numbers, Lawrence would run a custom-built script or program a special a spreadsheet, and it was done in an hour or two.

The old guys, Don and Rich, could only shake their heads and say, "How does he figure this shit out?"

His boss Grant slapped him on his arm and said, "You're our secret weapon."

Lawrence was the brightest star in the department and when he drove home through the city after working late, the Dog Star, the brightest, hardest-working star in the night sky, shone down between the buildings and through the windshield of his old Audi.

The bonuses were amazing. For two years in a row Lawrence made more in bonuses than he did in salary. And still he burned like the Dog Star. He moved his family from his apartment to a townhome in the city, then out of the city to Amberlaine, into a house with a driveway almost an eighth of a mile long in a neighborhood that overlooks Lake Michigan. A few months later, Lawrence traded in the Audi for an Tesla Model S, and that summer he bought a thirty-two foot Bayliner for cash.

What Lawrence failed to understand is that time and distance are the same thing. The Dog Star might be the brightest star in the night sky tonight, but eight-and-a-half light years away, the Dog Star could be collapsing on itself and it would be years before anyone notices.

Nowadays, Lawrence is lucky if he makes it to work by ten-thirty. The older guys Lawrence used to work into the ground six or seven years ago have moved on. Don quit and works part-time down at the marina now. Rich retired.

Nowadays, Grant says, "Lawrence, pay attention. I need you in the game here."

And there's a new crew of young guys. They don't carry briefcases. They don't use laptops. They do everything with their phones. They do things on their phones Lawrence can't even believe. And they can't believe Lawrence sits down at his computer to write scripts and populate spreadsheets.

"This is how I do it," Lawrence tells them. "I've been doing it this way for years."

"Yeah, exactly," they answer.

Lawrence's bonuses haven't dried up--not yet. He established some of the best accounts the company had ever seen, and his clients are more or less loyal. Fitzgerald would have to cut Lawrence several small bonus checks every year even if he slept at his desk all day.

But Lawrence isn't making nearly as much as he used to.

"I'm going to have keep the boat up here at the house this winter," Lawrence told Carrie last year. "Fees at the marina are going up, and I'm protesting."

"Right," said Carrie, "protesting."

"What's that supposed to mean?"

"Can you at least park it out on the circle drive and not next the house? It blocks the sun on my flowerbed."

To replace Don and Rich, Fitzgerald hired a young guy named Jeff, and he's working one-on-one with the department heads on a "Rationalization Plan" that's supposed to save the company a lot of money by making everyone more accountable for their time. Electronic, real-time time cards, daily billing.

Yesterday, Lawrence heard two guys from Production talking about it by the elevators.

The one said, "If that kid's plan works, I heard bonuses

are going up by six or seven percent."

The other said, "Oh, no doubt, but people're gonna get shit-canned before that happens. People who're dragging their feet, slacking. They gotta make sure everyone knows it's for real. Be glad that kid's not in our department. Be glad he doesn't know who we are."

Lawrence stares at them. They don't seem to notice.

It's probably better this way. Lawrence doesn't feel like the Dog Star anymore. He feels more like Orion, a spread-out collection of dimmer lights that look something like a man, if you squint and turn your head the right way. Now is Jeff's time. He's the Dog Star now, and Jeff is definitely feeling around for air leaks in the rubber boat. He's practically fondling it.

Technically, Lawrence has seniority, but Jeff doesn't seem too concerned with that. He might have been hired to be Orion's hunting companion, walking at the hunter's side, awaiting orders, but that's not how it worked out. Instead, the Dog Star follows Orion at a safe distance, watching, nipping at his heels.

***

Trent puts on his most serious face and gazes at himself in the bathroom mirror for something like three minutes. Black hair, black clothes, devastating dark expression.

And a big white pimple in the crease of his nose.

It throbs and tingles, so tumid that only a pin prick can relieve the pressure. Trent has a pin that would do it. He's got a sewing needle stuck in the wall next to the mirror for just this purpose. Trent just turned sixteen and his face is a constellation of such blemishes. Like stars, they burn hotter and hotter until they explode and collapse and then simmer.

When they're out in the open, like the one on his cheek the other day, Trent squeezes them between the black-painted nails of his index fingers, spattering the mirror with puss and pale blood. This leaves the bead of a scab that Trent can't help but pick off, which leaves a red crater that scabs over and gets picked again and so becomes a canker that festers, much worse than what was there at first.

His mother says, "Quit picking at it. You're just making it worse."

Trent doesn't listen. Instead he pushes his tongue hard against the inside of his mouth to keep the skin taut and scrapes the sore until an oily red paste collects under his fingernail.

His mother says, "Tell your son to quit picking."

His father says, "Trent. Quit picking."

His mother says, "He's making it worse.

His father says, "You're just making it worse."

It seems like that's the only thing his parents can agree about.

But Trent can't squeeze the pimple in the crease of his nose—too tender. It's only the size of a capital "o" on a page in the book that he is supposed to read for his ancient American Civ class, but it feels like it's big as a pencil eraser, or even a small marble, pressure building inside.

"What about Texas?" says his father at the dinner table.

"What about it?" says his mother. "It's hot. I wouldn't want to live there. Why are you looking at jobs, anyway? You have a job."

He shrugs. "What if something happens? What if I get laid off?"

"You're getting laid off?" She puts down her fork and looks at him. "When did this happen?"

"I'm not getting laid off," he says. "That's not what I said."

"That is what you said. You said, 'What if I get laid off?'"

"If we're moving," said Trent, "you need to just kill me." He gets up from the table.

"Stop it," says his dad.

"Stop what?" says Trent. "All I have is my friends. I can't have a car. Or even a job. I can't leave the house half the time."

"Bring your grades back up, then. Quit fagging around with those clowns you call friends. No more pot, no more trouble. Stop the weird hair, the make-up. Be respectful. Then we'll talk car. Then we'll talk job. Besides, nobody said we're moving."

Trent goes into his bathroom and locks the door.

"Come back here, Trent," his dad says as he goes. "This is what I'm talking about."

Trent looks at his face in the mirror. The pimple has become a tumor. A prick from the needle really would do the job, but last night the Pleiades peered into Trent's window as he read about the Black God of the native American tribes. The Black God, who got the seven stars of the Pleiades stuck in his foot as he came into his celestial hogan one night. When he stamped his foot to get rid of them, they only burrowed in deeper, like needles of tempered glass, until they lodged in his knee. So the Black God stamped again and they went all the way to his loins, which is not a place where you want a bunch of white hot needles of intergalactic crystal, so the Black God took a chance and stomped his foot a third time, and sure enough they drilled all the way to his shoulder, pointing directly at his heart. The fourth time the Black God stamped his foot, the needles ended up in his face, just an inch or so from his brain, and finally the Black God set his hogan on fire, and to this day he sits inside as it burns and burns in the night sky forever.

***

A Portuguese navigator on a ship full of copper and ivory from Sierra Leone would keep his eye on the Polestar all night long. As the ship sailed north out of the tropics, the Polestar would appear to rise higher and higher each night, owing to the ship's position higher and higher on the globe. When their crude navigational instruments showed the Polestar standing thirty-nine degrees above the dark horizon, they steered the ship east for their homes in Lisbon. If a storm tossed the ship off course and they got lost, or if sky were shrouded in clouds, the Portuguese sailors never blamed the Polestar. The Polestar is fixed, the only celestial body in the Earthly sky that never moves.

Carrie blusters into the bedroom and says, "What are these doing here?"

"They're socks," says Lawrence.

He's on the bed watching television. He was going to watch the news channel to find out what the market did today, but he got distracted by a history program on early sea exploration.

"I know they're socks," says Carrie. "What are they doing on the floor?"

She picks them up and turns them outside-right. She turns all the laundry outside-right before putting it in the hamper.

"I suppose they're doing what socks do after you take them off—talking about their day, maybe. Or maybe they just need fifteen minutes to unwind. If that's the case, tell them I know exactly how they feel."

"I'm sick of picking up after everyone."

"I just took them off. I just walked in the door."

"Why are you so late?"

"I stopped to get bread. You told me to get bread for dinner."

"I already went and got the bread," she says.

"Then why did you tell me to get it? You know it's out of my way. Why tell me to get it if you're going to get it yourself?"

"I assumed you'd forget."

"But I didn't forget."

"That's not my fault," she says.

She makes a good point.

"Could've called me," he says, but she's gone. She has his socks.

Lawrence turns up the television. He knows the Polestar isn't motionless. It only looks that way because the Earth's axis happens to point in that direction. And even the Polestar wobbles slightly because it doesn't line up exactly with the Earth, but Lawrence doesn't have instruments sensitive enough to detect the wobble, he can't prove it, and he grows tired of gazing into the black.

Besides, he's got a meeting with his boss tomorrow. It's at

10 a.m. Grant told him three times to be there on time.

"It's just me, you, and Jeff, okay? So none of this slouching in twenty minutes late. I want to start at ten sharp."

Lawrence knows he'll be fired. He can feel it. Jeff has shown them the air leaks in the rubber boat. Tomorrow is Jeff's day. He's the Dog Star now.

Lawrence stands up and crosses the bedroom to his bureau. In the bottom drawer, there is a revolver. He picks it up. It's heavy. Lawrence hefts its before opening the briefcase and slides the revolver inside. He sets the briefcase in the hallway by the garage door.

***

Lawrence checks his phone as he arrives at Fitzgerald. It's five minutes after ten. He turns the phone off and pockets it. The conference room door is ajar. Grant and Jeff are inside, seated already at the conference table. They're talking, smiling. Jeff laughs.

Lawrence pushes the door open, an apology and excuse for his lateness forming in his mind.

"But why?" thinks Lawrence. "Why in the goddam hell would I apologize to anyone today?"

"Hey, Lawrence," says Jeff, a little too loudly. "How are you, sir?"

"I'm good, Jeff. In fact," adds Lawrence, his face an expressionless mask, "I'm better than good. I'm fucking phenomenal."

Jeff and Grant trade a look. "Well," says Jeff, "that's good."

"Have a seat," says Grant.

Lawrence sits across the conference table from them. He places the briefcase on its side on the chair next to him. The zippered mouth of the case is open. He slides his hand inside. The revolver is not there. Wrong pocket? He feels around.

"Well, there's no sense dicking around here, Lawrence, so let's just jump right in."

"Sure," says Lawrence. His hand goes into another pocket. The revolver is not there.

Jeff leans forward in his chair, puts his arms on the table, and grins.

"You know we're making some big changes, right?" says Grant. "I know nothing's been said officially, but you've heard things, right?"

"Sure." His hand is probing the pockets. The pistol is not there.

"Right," says Grant. "Well, as you've probably guessed, we're going forward with a sleeker team, fewer people."

"Sure." The gun is not in the case.

"I'm stepping down," says Grant. "I'm retiring."

"Retiring? You?"

"Ah, c'mon, man." Grant chuckles. "You don't have to play dumb for me. It's time. I love this company, but it's time for me to step aside. And don't play dumb when I tell you it's time for you to step up."

"Step up. Step up to--"

"You're taking the reins of the department, Lawrence. Obviously."

Jeff nods and grins.

Lawrence withdraws his hand from the case. He blinks a few times, turns to face Jeff and says, "So, Jeff--"

"I'm working for you now, sir," says Jeff. "And I'm super excited. I admire the hell out of your work. Always have."

"Lawrence changed everything when he got here," says Grant fondly, jabbing a thumb in Lawrence's direction. "Everyone knows that. Transformed our whole operation."

"I've seen the numbers," says Jeff, still nodding. "I've seen the data."

***

That night, after an interminable series of meetings that Lawrence remembers almost nothing about, he gets into the Tesla and drives out of the city. The sky is free of clouds, and the Dog Star gazes down at him as he speeds along the toll way. Twenty minutes later he takes his exit and eases onto Lakeside Boulevard.

"My god," he says. "My god." He says it over and over.

He shakes his head.

In the rearview mirror, Lawrence's eye catches the twinkle of cop car lights. He quails, instinctively lifting his foot from the accelerator, thinking of the gun which is not in the briefcase that he did not use to kill anyone. But it's not a police car. It's a fire truck. It races on by.

The pay increase Grant offhandedly proposed had almost made Lawrence choke, and he'd be getting five percent of every finder's fee in the department. He'd need a calculator to even make a guess at what that would mean.

"My god."

When Lawrence reaches the turn-off to the driveway to his house, he pulls the Tesla onto the shoulder of the road and puts the car in park. He pushes a button to activate the dome light. Then he takes his briefcase from the passenger's seat and sets it upright on his lap. With a urgent deliberateness, Lawrence empties the case and shoves his hands down into each of the pockets, baffling them wide open and searching. Then he sets the case on the passenger seat. He stares out the windshield for a while before turning down the driveway.

As Lawrence nears the house, the bluish headlights glare against the shaggy pine trees and the looming white oaks. But through the trees comes a harsher light, the furious orange of an enormous fire, and the blue and red strobes of emergency vehicles.

Out on the gravel circle drive, the Bayliner is gloriously ablaze. The flames are at least forty feet tall, and the hot, upwelling draft causes the branches of the nearby trees to bob and sway as they catch fire, too.

The massive craft looks like a bright and gleaming funeral ship. It rests on its Sea Tech triple-axle aluminum trailer, the bow slightly but majestically inclined upward, dwarfing the scrambling firefighters in their baggy, reflective over clothes.

The house is also on fire.

***

Locked in his bathroom, as the oily black smoke of flaming carpet roils up under the door, the Black God presses he cool muzzle of a revolver to his face, placing it directly over a seething white blemish in the crease of his nose.

KELLER HALL
Amanda Luzzader

I could see the parking lot from my window three stories up. I'd been trying so hard to not let them see me getting emotional. I kept my back to Dad as he carried in box after box of my stuff into the freshly painted dorm room. I turned away as Mom help me unpack my dinner plates and cereal bowls.

"You gonna be all right, hon?" my mom asked me, putting my towels in a closet.

I could only nod. Just saying one word would have cracked me. Maybe they knew how scared I was, but I couldn't let them see it.

From the window, I watched Dad's old truck pulling away. Now that they were gone, I couldn't bear it anymore and I started crying.

Applying at Kensington had been my idea, one Mom and Dad had objected to at first.

"Why not just apply to U of O?" Dad said. "You could keep living here, ride your bike to class. Kensington's a twelve-hour drive."

"Yeah, hon," said Mom. "And you don't know anyone there. Everyone you know is here. All your friends are here."

Right. All two of them.

They were right, though. They knew how socially backward I am, how hard it is for me even to meet people, let alone make friends. I'd had a hard enough time just with high school. I'd started a nobody and graduated a nobody. I thought Kensington could be my chance to change everything. To reinvent myself. Still, it took a lot of effort to even consider the idea. The scholarships had helped—I had nearly everything paid for. But I knew Mom and Dad worried about me. And now I was pretty worried, too.

I touched my hand to the cool window pane. What made me think I could survive here? What made me think this place would be different than high school? Or the rest of my life? I had two friends in high school—Maddy and Victoria. Together we'd made it to graduation, gotten this far in life, and I loved them, but I was by myself now. Victoria got a scholarship to U of O, and Maddy was practically engaged. Sure, we could text sometimes, chat online. And I'd see them on breaks, maybe. But for the rest of the time I had no one. My mom, dad, friends, brothers—they were all hours away now, and they all their own lives and problems. I didn't know one single person at Kensington. I didn't want to be alone.

I pulled out my cell phone. This had all been a big a mistake. There was still time. I could leave Kensington, skip this semester, apply to U of O, and start in the winter. Mom would understand. Dad would turn around and come get me. We'd load my stuff into his truck again and I could be back at home tomorrow.

But just as I found Mom's number in my contacts, a girl walked past my dorm room door, down the hallway, and out of sight.

I hadn't heard her or anything. I didn't know there was anyone else on the entire floor. She was suddenly just there as my finger hovered over the *call* button.

I wiped my eyes, hoping that she wouldn't be able to tell I'd been crying. I pocketed the phone and then went to find her.

The dorm consisted of two private bedrooms, shared bathroom, small kitchen, and a living room. I went down the hall and found the girl in the other bedroom. She had boxes piled all around her. How long had she been there? Why hadn't I noticed? Her bed was lifted up on cinder blocks and she was playing Souxsie and the Banshees. Kind of a really old band, but I liked it.

I stood at her doorway for a minute, but she didn't seem to notice I was there, so I knocked on the open door.

"Hi," I said softly.

"Oh, hey," she said. "You must be my roommate! Last I heard they were still looking for another placement."

"Yeah, that's what they told me, too. I'm Liz."

Her name was Rachel, and it was her first year at Kensington, also. She was pretty. She had long dark hair, dark eyes, and pale skin. She was striking, and I might have thought she'd be really unrelatable, but she was super friendly and we had no trouble making conversation. It seemed as though she had a million things to say.

"I'm sorry I keep talking so much," said Rachel. "I'm usually not so chatty. I don't know what's wrong with me. Guess it's been kind of a long, slow summer. Haven't really had anyone to talk to in forever."

"It's okay," I said. "Better than being quiet all the time, like me."

I helped Rachel set up her room, since mine was already done. She had lots of candles and weird little statues of angels. When we finished we went into the living room and started up an unplanned *Gilmore Girls* marathon. Rachael said she didn't have any food yet, but I had a whole case of microwave popcorn. We didn't go to bed until after midnight.

Lying in my bed in the strange dorm room, I didn't feel alone anymore. I had one friend. That's half the number I had all through high school, and that would be enough for now. I thought about Mom and Dad. I couldn't call them now—they were probably back at home already. As I drifted off to sleep, I thought maybe I'd wait until Christmas break, then re-evaluate.

Now that I had a friend, it seemed like anything was possible.

On Tuesdays and Thursday evenings, Rachel was usually gone—she said she had evenings classes. She'd be gone at other times, too, but I was too shy to ask where she went. I studied a lot on weeknights, anyway, and I usually went to bed early. But Friday nights Rachel was home and we made a kind of tradition of watching either a horror move or chick flick. We called it our "Moaning Movies Night." We watched Alfred Hitchcock's *Vertigo*. We watched *Ghost* and *Sabrina*.

One Friday night I came home to the dorm, excited for a good moaning movie. I'd been studying for a stats exam all week and I was ready for a break. Plus, it was getting dark so early now—even though I loved scary movies, the dark, blustery campus was unsettling somehow. It was gusty outside, and the dry autumn leaves drifted and rattled ominously on the wind.

Once inside the dorm, I picked out a movie and popped the popcorn. We usually started the moaning movies around seven o'clock and it was barely six-thirty, but we introverts are creatures of habits, so I got everything ready and then waited on the couch. I read a little Econ 1010, and then I went over some class notes until seven.

But Rachel didn't show.

I figured she'd gotten held up somewhere and was running late, so I read some more. Seven-thirty—no Rachel. Eight, eight-thirty, nine—no Rachel. By the time ten o'clock rolled around, I was really worried. I didn't want to be clingy or naggy, but I decided to call her. It was either that or call the campus police.

But I couldn't find Rachel's number in my contacts list. I'd been living practically side-by-side with Rachel all semester, so I guess we hadn't talked on the phone or texted yet, and I hadn't put her in my phone. I couldn't remember Rachel even giving me her number. I apparently hadn't written it down, either, or maybe in my panic I couldn't find it. My stomach felt queasy. I thought it'd be best to call the police, but I was so unsure—Rachel was a grown woman, and we had never actually set a formal date or time for Moaning Movie Nights. They just sort of happened. So, what if I called the police and Rachel walked in a few minutes later? What if she was just away for the weekend? I didn't have much experience with friends—what was the right thing to do here?

I paced up and down my bedroom, but kept checking my phone. Surely I'd given her my number—maybe she'd text me. Did I know anyone from classes or study groups who knew her? I got so worried.

After another hour, I decided to go look for her. Maybe she was at the student center studying or at the coffee place by the library. I put on my coat and hat. Then I decided it'd be a good idea to leave a note, in case Rachel came back while I was gone. I went to the kitchen and got a pen and paper, and just as I wrote her name, I heard sounds from her bedroom.

I hadn't even heard her come in.

I stormed into her room. "Rachel, my god!"

She shrieked.

"Where have you been?" I yelled.

"I was out, Liz!" she shouted. "God! You almost scared me to death. I was out with some friends. I'm just here to change clothes and I'm headed back out."

"I was worried about you. I tried to call you, but I realized I don't even know your phone number."

"Why would you be worried about me?" She pulled on a baggy black sweater, glanced in the mirror, and then put on a black beret.

"I thought we were gonna watch a movie tonight. Like we do. I picked out a good one. *Lady in White.*"

"Oh. Moaning Movies. I forgot. But we can watch a movie anytime. I gotta go."

"Where are you going?"

"Jeeze. What's with the third degree? I'm sick of being in this dorm. It gives me the creeps. I'm going to the Black Cow for drinks. Why do you want to know? I said we'll watch a movie some other night."

"Maybe I could come with you."

I pictured myself going out. I knew people "went out for drinks" to meet friends and have fun. People in TV shows did it, in movies, in books. I pictured myself there with Rachel. Everyone else probably already else would know each other. I'd be the outsider, flitting around the margins of the fun—a wallflower, a phantom, practically invisible. I hate crowds. I hate loud places. Was it really so bad that I'd rather a night at home with Netflix or a good book than hang around at some dimly lit bar that reeked of body odor and beer? Still, Rachel was my friend, and I'd decided that with a friend, anything might be possible.

"Have you been in my room?" Rachel asked bluntly.

"Your room? No. Why?"

"I don't know. You're sure? You haven't opened the window? Or moved any of my things around?"

"No, of course not."

She scowled at me.

"So, would it be okay if I tagged along?" I asked.

"I don't know. Maybe not this time. I'm meeting a friend."

"Oh."

"Some other time," she said. "We'll go out some other time." She scooted around me in the small bedroom and made her way to the door without turning her back to me.

"Have a good time," I said.

But she came to our movie nights less and less, until finally they seemed to be a thing of the past. Rachel would be suddenly gone from the apartment—sometimes for days. Did she really think I'd been in her room? But I saw her so infrequently I sometimes thought I had only imagined her. Was that possible? Could I just imagine an entire person? An entire roommate? When she did come to the apartment, we seldom spoke, and sometimes it was like she wasn't even there.

I hadn't made any other friends. I was too shy and there were just so many students. And I was hurt that Rachel had seemed to dispose of me so easily, so I was cagey, nervous. Maybe next semester would be better. I could get a new roommate, maybe meet some new people.

Still, I thought, I should at least try to work things out with Rachel.

She'd been gone for three or four days. Maybe more. The days were so dark and gray then. They seemed to go by so fast that sometimes I thought I'd lost track of time. One morning I heard the fridge open. I went to the kitchen speak with her.

When she saw me, she slammed the fridge shut and folded her arms.

"Don't talk to me," she said.

"Rachel, why? What's changed between us? I thought we were friends."

"Friends? You don't think I know about you? Who you are? And what about you and this John guy? I've heard all about it. It's just my dumb luck that I'd get placed in this dorm. I've already made a request to transfer. Just leave me alone until it goes through. I'm warning you. Stay away from me. And quit going into my room!"

I had no idea what she was talking about.

"I don't understand. What have you heard? And I've never gone into your room!"

"Stay away from me!"

She grabbed her purse from where she'd left it on the couch and left in a hurry, slamming the door behind her.

It was just like high school, I thought. Always being the outsider and all the girls making up lies about me to keep me out. Hating me for reasons I could never understand. Now I'd moved clear across the state to escape, but here I was again. Who was John? What was this about Rachel's room?

I was done trying to make friends with Rachel, or anyone else, really. I didn't need her. I didn't need anyone.

After that, I saw even less of Rachel. A couple times I thought I heard her crying in the night, but I just put my pillow over my ears. She wasn't my problem anymore. She'd slam doors and cabinets a lot—sometimes in the middle of the night, sometimes when I hadn't even known she was home. I think just to annoy or frighten me, but otherwise it didn't bother me much. I stayed in my room and she stayed in hers.

Then, one night, around 3 a.m., I woke up. I'm not sure why—I must have heard them coming in. I sat in bed and listened. Someone was moving around in the kitchen or living room. I heard a man's laughter, then shushing, then more laughing. Someone was definitely out there. I held my breath, straining to hear. I heard whispering. I heard footsteps getting closer.

My door burst open. The light came on. Three people came into my room. The first of them was a college boy, tall and broad with blond hair. He looked like he might be on the football team, but he held a baseball bat, so maybe not. He was definitely burly and strong, and under other circumstances, I would have thought he was handsome. The other boy was thin but wiry. He had his phone held up like he was video taping.

Coming in behind the two boys was Rachel.

"There she is!" hissed Rachel. Rachel's mascara had run down her face, as though she'd been crying for a long time. She looked weak and pale, as if she maybe hadn't been sleeping. And she'd staggered like she was pretty drunk.

The wiry guy looked at his phone and thrust it forward toward me.

"God," he said. "She looks so real."

"She's not!" said Rachel, her voice shaky.

"Get out! Get out! Get out!" I screamed, scooting back into the corner of my bed and pulling the blanket up to my chin. "What are you doing?"

"I know what you are, Liz," sobbed Rachel. She had a crazed look in her eyes.

The three of them stayed close together. Their eyes were glassy and cheeks red. They'd all been drinking, obviously, or they were super high. The burly one held the bat like he might hit me with it if I made a false move. The other was taping with his phone, narrating everything he saw in a wildly over-dramatic voice.

"This is the real-life ghost of Keller Hall, Elizabeth, who killed herself and her boyfriend John in this very dorm eight years ago, and who now haunts the students who live here."

"Rachel make them stop! You're scaring me."

"Scaring you?" said Rachel. "You've been harassing me for months. Moving my things in the night! Slamming doors! Making stuff float around!" She was hysterical.

"What? No!" I said.

"Then who keeps coming into my room and stands there staring at me? And that horrid face in my mirror! You're dead! You're the dead girl! You're a ghost!"

"Rachel, you're completely wasted! Can't you see how crazy this all sounds! I didn't do anything to you, I promise! Stop this right now!"

The two boys had gotten very close to me. The wiry one was transfixed by my image on his phone. The burly guy was trying to poke me with the bat, but his depth perception was obviously quite impaired. I tried pushing them back and jumped out of bed. Rachel screamed. The boys reeled back, apparently shocked that I was fighting back.

All three of them seemed terrified now. They backed up against my bedroom door. Rachel was holding her head in both hands, sobbing. The two men again began drunkenly closing in on me again.

"Do something! Do something, Landon!" Rachel wailed at them, pointing at me. "I can't take it anymore!"

"What can I do?" the burly guy shouted. "She's not really there! What can I—"

"Landon, do something!" Rachel shrieked again.

Landon raised the bat over his head and charged.

I backed up a step or two, but he kept coming. When he slammed into me, it felt like I'd been hit by a rhino. I flew back like a doll and we both toppled into the window behind me.

Everything happened slowly. I felt my back impact the window, felt the window give way, shattering, splintering. I felt the cold air outside, saw the twinkling glass shards and the icy stars in the sky. I saw the broken window of my dorm room from the outside. I saw Rachel screaming. The wiry guy kept taping. I saw the burly guy's face—eyes bulging and mouth open in horror.

We fell.

I heard sirens. There were EMTs, strobing lights. There were students in sweats and no shoes standing around on the sidewalks, looking, pointing, crying. I heard someone say "tragic," and someone else said "MDMA," and someone said "acid trip." They brought Rachel out of Keller Hall. She was thrashing, shrieking. It took two men to handle her. They took her away in a police car. Someone put a blanket over me, but I seemed to be seeing it all happen from above, from below, from all sides. They put me in the ambulance and the ambulance drove out of the parking lot without its siren on. I watched it all, but in a detached way. I felt agitated, odd, untethered. A fiercely white light blazed in the darkness somewhere behind me, and I turned to it, but something told me I couldn't go there. Not yet. Not yet.

The next thing I remember is sitting on the couch in the living room of my dorm. The Netflix menu displayed warmly on the TV, and a pretty girl with sandy red hair sat to my right. I turned to face her.

"Hi," she said.

"Hello," I said. "I'm Liz."

"I know. My name's Elizabeth, too," she said. "But I go by Beth."

"Oh," I said. "Cool."

The air had a thin feeling, and the room itself had a strange, static quality, as though time had stopped passing. I myself felt odd and incomplete.

After a moment or two, she said, "You get used to it after a while."

"Okay," I said. "Thanks."

"I'm really sorry about what happened," said Beth.

"What do you mean?"

"Rachel's a real bitch," the girl said.

I nodded.

"I was only trying to make her move out," said Beth. "Because I think I know how you are. Quiet, shy. Like me. I knew you wouldn't get along with Rachel. I was only trying to get you a new roommate. I had no idea she'd go nuts. I didn't think you'd ever end up—well, you know—here, with me."

I nodded again. We sat in silence for a while. Time passed but it didn't.

"But I hope we can be friends," said Beth.

"Do you like Gilmore Girls?" I asked.

"Oh, I love it. It's my favorite."

I smiled. "Then I think we can be friends."

Beth nodded.

"You know," I said, "sometimes I think if you just have one good friend, anything's possible."

Beth nodded and grinned. "Well, I have good news, then."

"What?"

"You actually have two friends," she said, pointing.

I turned around to look, and sitting on the other side of the couch was a burly guy with blond hair. He was handsome.

"Hey," he said, waving to us. "I'm Landon."

FUEL STATION
RESTROOM, 11:05 P.M.
Chadd VanZanten

Her body was wedged between the toilet and the partition. The boy first saw her legs, hyper-extended and sprawling from the stall out into plain sight, but that's not what frightened him most.

"Yeah, go ahead," his dad had said when the boy told him he needed to pee. "I'll be in the car."

The boy next noticed the dark spreading pool on the floor beneath her knees, pooling up and settling into the grout around the hexagonal tiles. But that was not the most terrible thing, either, though the boy had never seen such a quantity of that substance in one place, at one time.

What frightened him most was the thick-bodied fellow at the sink who turned off the faucet as the boy entered, the watery red droplets on the bright porcelain, and the wink he gave as he approached without drying his hands.

About the Authors

Amanda Luzzader writes science fiction, horror, and thriller stories. Most recently, she published a dystopian thriller called *Among These Bones* in 2018. Amanda will be releasing *When It's No Longer Night* in late 2018. She is a self-described 'fraidy cat. Things she will run away from include (but are not limited to): mice, snakes, spiders, bits of string and litter that resemble spiders, most members of the insect kingdom, and (most especially) bats. Bats are the worst. But Amanda is first and primarily a mother to two energetic and intelligent sons. Amanda has worked as a technical writer and a professional editor and is currently employed as a grant writer for a Utah nonprofit organization. She is a devout cat person.

Chadd VanZanten's short stories have appeared in numerous anthologies and publications, including *It Came from the Great Salt Lake* (Griffin Publishers), *Volatile When Mixed* (LUW Press), and *The Helicon West Anthology* (Helicon West Press). He also writes outdoor essays and is the author of *On Fly-Fishing the Wind River Range* and co-author of *On Fly-Fishing the Northern Rockies* (both released by The History Press). Chadd is a professional editor and loves hiking and fly-fishing but could never get enough of binge-watching Netflix with his best friend, writing partner, wife, and muse, Amanda.

For more information or to sign up for her newsletter, visit:
www.amandaluzzader.com.

You can also follow us on Facebook:
www.facebook.com/authoramandaluzzader/
www.facebook.com/onflyfishing

Check out our other books!

AMONG THESE BONES

Alison and her son Arie survived a global pandemic along with a remnant of humanity, but the annual cure that keeps them alive also steals their memories. The harsh rule of a shadowy governing organization known as The Agency is grim enough, but Alison's world is torn apart when Arie goes missing. Alison joins a team of resistance fighters to uncover the truth, but if she can't find Arie before she has to take the serum again, she won't remember she even has a son.

ON FLY-FISHING THE WIND RIVER RANGE

With remote waterways and unpressured trout, Wyoming's Wind River Range is the backcountry fly angler's mecca. In the alpine lakes and streams, trout may approach a dry fly two or more at a time, and an angler can cast for days without seeing another angler. But more than just a place to catch lots of fish, the range is also a place to disconnect from noise and networks and reconnect with oneself. In essays on misfortunate backpacking trips, disaffected Boy Scouts, and psychotropic deep-woods epiphanies, Chadd VanZanten offers not only a survey of the fishing and history of the Wind Rivers but a tour of personal landscapes as well.

ON FLY-FISHING THE NORTHERN ROCKIES

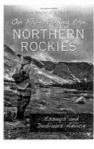

Fly-fishing the West is liberating, poetic, wild, soothing. In essays ranging from introspective to ironic, Chadd VanZanten and Russ Beck distill the truths of fly-fishing into essential and humorous rules of thumb such as "always tell the truth sometimes" and "all the fish are underwater." Wade into the blue ribbon waters of Montana, Idaho, Wyoming and Utah to reflect metaphysically on these lines of practical wisdom.

Made in the USA
Las Vegas, NV
04 February 2022

43092575R00069